"SYBELLA, WHAT IS IT?"

Gripping her shaking shoulders, he struggled to comfort her. But she fought him desperately.

"Please!" she begged. "Please don't hurt me!"

"Hurt you! You little fool!" Then his mouth was hard upon hers, his arms crushing her tightly against the lean length of his body. "I love you," he whispered. "God knows I would never harm you."

He held her from him and looked close into her tear-filled eyes. "You do believe that, don't you?"

But how could Sybella believe him? Ever since she met Adam Brady, her very life had been in mortal danger . . . !

*Also by Maye Barrett
from Jove*

THE THORN IN THE ROSE

The Threat of Love

MAYE BARRETT

A JOVE BOOK

Requests for permission to make copies of any part
of the work should be mailed to: Permissions,
Jove Publications, Inc., 200 Madison Avenue,
New York, NY 10016

First Jove edition published November 1980

10 9 8 7 6 5 4 3 2 1

Printed in the United States of America

Jove books are published by Jove Publications, Inc.,
200 Madison Avenue, New York, NY 10016

Chapter One

"I won't marry him!" With a savage sweep of her wrist Sybella Howard sent a tortoiseshell box of satin hair ribbons sailing high into the air. Then she flung herself down upon the fragile little chair in front of the dressing table and stared angrily back at her own reflection.

In any mood the reflected face was a beautiful one. The eyes, more green than hazel, were wide-set beneath slim, arched brows, and the hair, a myriad of loose curls confined in front by a yellow ribbon, was coal black. A connoisseur of feminine charms in the Napoleonic era might possibly have considered the mouth a trifle overgenerous in such a delicately small face, the eyes perhaps too slanted, or the jaw just a trifle too square, but the overall effect, if not traditionally beautiful, was, to say the least, arresting.

In the top right-hand corner of the mirror Sophie Servais bobbed nervously, her soft, plump features clouding apprehensively at her niece's sudden outburst.

"Oh, my dear, please don't take on so." Her voice was so light it seemed a sudden breeze might whisk it away forever and it matched exactly her middle-aged prettiness which the modishly unstinted application of white greasepaint and Serkisrouge had unfortunately made just a trifle too flamboyant. "At least not just now," she pleaded feebly. "The guests are certain to arrive within the hour and those wretched musicians downstairs are still unable to produce a noise that even remotely resembles the new valse tempo I wanted so much to have." Her face crumpled miserably. "Just listen to them! And on top of it all cook is sulking because I ordered all those pistachio nuts and sugared mushrooms from Berthelots! Really, I only did it because I thought she had so much to do already."

Temporarily sidetracked by the exhausting pressures of Sybella's farewell ball, Sophie lost the gist of her immediate problem and unmindfully cast about in her reticule for her vinaigrette whilst Sybella watched her performance with growing impatience.

"Aunt Sophie, will you please listen to me? I won't marry him, and the instant I return to England I shall tell him so!"

"Oh dear, oh dear child!" Sophie gave up the unequal battle with her reticule and wondered

2

distractedly if indeed she had not gone far beyond the healing properties of smelling salts anyway. She pressed her fingers to her temples and addressed the back of Sybella's head hopefully. "If only, my dear, you would allow yourself to consider this matter quietly and diligently."

"I have considered it! I have considered nothing else these past twelve hours ever since Uncle Philippe told me Julian had asked for my hand and he had given it. Now I have made up my mind and no additional amount of quiet nor diligent consideration shall ever make me change it."

"Sybella, dear, you are being disrespectful."

"Then I am truly sorry, Aunt Sophie, for I have no mind to be."

For one brief instant Sophie wondered why fate was being so viciously unkind to her. Yet, as she regarded Sybella's straight little back, so rigidly defiant, she still could not banish the cheering thought that tomorrow the child's visit would be at an end and she would be well on her way back to England. Through the heavy green velvet curtaining of the windows the life of Paris filtered softly.

Sybella stirred and Sophie waited cautiously, watching the long, slender fingers beat a mild tattoo on the top of the dressing table. Then with an abrupt change of mood that sent Sophie scurrying to her side, Sybella swung round to face her aunt, the green eyes sparkling with unshed tears.

"Oh, Aunt Sophie, why is it so desirable that

3

I marry Cousin Julian?''

With a sigh that could have been interpreted as being either one of sympathy or relief, Sophie gave her niece a conciliatory hug and drew up a chair beside her.

"Because, my child, this marriage is not only for your own good, it is also a really most admirable match and, you know, your cousin loves you very much.''

"I don't love him.''

"That doesn't signify." Sophie dismissed this assertion with a touch of irritability. "Just think on this. You will be Lady Sybella Rivers. You will be the mistress of a twenty-roomed house and the wife of a highly regarded and most presentable man who has known and adored you since the day you were born. I am certain your dear parents would have been as delighted as your uncle and I am. Never forget, Sybella, it was your parents, you know, who entrusted him to be your guardian, and but for him, my dear child, I dare not even contemplate what would have become of you during all those awful years of trouble between our countries when we could do nothing for you. It really makes me feel quite undone to even mention it!'' She sighed into the mirror and patted her hair absently before continuing. "Now the war is over, your Uncle Philippe has been very clever with money matters but we are still not yet rich, so you can surely see why we are so happy that you are going to be well taken care of by Julian.''

Sybella's eyes glinted dangerously. "You make

4

it sound as if I should be grateful for the opportunity of marrying the first man with money who speaks for me!''

Sophie chose her words carefully before she answered. "Frankly, my dear, yes—you should."

"What!" Sybella stared at her incredulously. "Aunt Sophie, surely you can't mean that I should sell myself?"

"I hardly think we need drag commerce into the conversation, dear," Sophie answered somewhat testily. "We were discussing the honourable proposal of marriage from a man who loves you."

"But whom I don't love—so it amounts to the same thing! And for what reason? I'm not exactly a pauper. I realize I know next to nothing about money matters, but surely the investments my father left me will continue on in the future and I have always managed creditably well in the past."

Sophie took a deep breath and wriggled uncomfortably in her chair before replying. She frowned distastefully and took hold of Sybella's hand kindly. "My dear, it is high time you were told the truth." She averted her eyes from her niece's flushed face and hurried on. "I am afraid, Sybella, that for many years past your allowance has owed a great deal more to Julian's own pocket and kindness of heart than it could ever owe to any business genius of your dear father. I'm sorry, my child."

Sybella shook her head. "He should have told me," she whispered.

"Not at all! You are much too pretty to have had to think about such matters! But now, we must be practical. In three months you come of age and after that you can no longer expect Julian's protection as a right. Now, don't you see why it is such a stroke of good fortune that he should wish to make you his wife?" She squeezed Sybella's hands reassuringly. "You are a very lucky girl and with good common-sense you can also be a very happy one." She tilted her head to one side in a listening attitude before suddenly leaping to her feet with an excited little squeal. "My dear, just listen— they're waltzing! Oh my, what a wonderful evening it has turned out after all!" She hugged Sybella effusively. "Come now, you must finish your toilet and so must I." She was already at the door calling for Sybella's abigail. "Beatrice! Your mistress needs you! Hurry!"

For minutes after her aunt had left the room, Sybella remained motionless in a frantic endeavour to control her whirling thoughts. She was penniless, she told herself over and over again and, apart from Julian Rivers, completely at the mercy of a world she knew less about than the lowliest serving wench. Her stomach churned sickeningly and instead of her mind clearing, she felt it growing more and more confused. Finally she could stand it no longer and she gratefully surrendered herself to the destiny her aunt and uncle had sensibly prepared for her.

"Lady Sybella Rivers." She forced dry lips to frame the name and then said it twice more, softly, as if repetition alone would convince her of its desirability. She picked up her hairbrush and drew it thoughtfully through her black curls. As the wife of Julian Rivers she would enjoy a life similar to the one she had always known and always expected. That he loved her she had no doubt. He was a good man she felt sure, and as her friend and guardian she had always respected him, but the possibility of marriage had never occurred to her. She paused in her absentminded toilet and allowed a mental picture of Julian to flash before her eyes. His long, rather thin face with its highly accentuated cheekbones and alert brown eyes was not necessarily unattractive to any girl, even one half his age. For an instant Sybella wondered then at her own distaste until she remembered the thin, straight line of his mouth and heard the sarcasm he kept reserved in his voice. The hand holding the hairbrush stayed suspended in midair, and she was unaware of anything except the image of Julian Rivers and the burning crimson in her cheeks that was slowly stealing over her whole body.

"Satan's oven!" she hissed her most vehement oath through clenched teeth. "I'll marry the devil himself first before I sell myself to Julian Rivers or anybody else!" And the future? The future could take care of itself, later, she told herself.

She appeared quite calm when Beatrice Crewe arrived five minutes later to help her with her dressing. Jumping to her feet as the tall, elderly woman entered, Sybella took hold of her by both hands and dragged her unceremoniously into the centre of the room. "Beatie, do you realize that I am still only half dressed?" Her voice was gently teasing as she surveyed her fondly. "I expect you have been practising the valse?"

"Humph!" With a withering sniff she propelled a bony hand smartly against the girl's bottom and briskly crossed to the wardrobe.

Beatrice Crewe was a woman in her mid-fifties. Thin, almost to the point of emaciation, she was, nevertheless, as tough as leather. Her long face, with its permanent expression of complete distaste, was made droll by an expressive nose that could sniff more deprecatingly than the greatest orator could have equalled in words, and when she did speak, her voice was as dry as a wood chip. Only her eyes, small and very blue, could ever betray her—and they were invariably twinkling. Unfortunately, few people knew it. She had become abigail to Sybella's mother the same day the little French bride had arrived in London after her runaway marriage with her youthful English lover. She had become one of the family then, and when they had died in a carriage wreck barely twelve months after Sybella's birth, she had adopted the role of foster mother, nursemaid, and abigail. Nobody had asked her and nobody would have dared try to stop her. In that capacity she had lived ever since.

The trunks had almost all been filled in preparation for the next day's journey and the wardrobe was empty except for the ball dress. Sybella watched idly as the gown was laid out upon the bed.

"Aunt Sophie declares that when the valse is danced correctly, the gentleman holds his partner so close to him that at times a knife edge cannot be placed between them," she remarked conversationally.

"Sybella, kindly hush such talk this instant!"

"Well, it is true—that is what she said!" She slipped out of her peignoir and stood in her lace-trimmed drawers, ready to dress.

"I have no time to dispute your aunt's wealth of information," Beatie assured her acidly. "However I must say I find it shameful that this dance was ever allowed to leave the Palais Royal—where it undoubtedly originated."

"Beatie!" Sybella pretended to be shocked but the mention of the notorious Palais Royal was too much for her to ignore. "Beatie, is it really as scandalous as they say? Have you ever been there? I am sure all the men I have met have been there but they will not admit it, and the very first week we were here I overheard Uncle Philippe give directions to his coachman to go there. What do you think really goes on that is so wicked? I mean apart from the usual things that men want—"

"Sybella!" Beatie broke in with swift admonition. "That is sufficient. All this talk is of no accord. Now, put on your chemise before you catch an ill."

9

Sybella took no notice. Instead she crossed to the full-length mirror and stood before it.

"Tell me honestly, do you think my figure is sufficiently developed to interest men like that?" She took a deep breath and thrust out her small, firm breasts voluptuously.

"Great heavens, what are you saying now?" This time Beatie was truly shocked. "I swear I don't know what has taken hold of you. Three weeks in this heathen country has stripped you of every modesty. Come, put on your chemise this instant!"

In silence Sybella allowed the garment to be slipped over her head.

"I have a reason for asking you."

"I prefer not to hear it."

"Truly, I am only asking because I need your advice."

"Be still!"

She waited impatiently for the twenty-four tiny seed-pearl buttons to be fastened at the back of her ball gown, a charming buttercup yellow crepe splashed from bodice to hem with powder blue velvet ribbons spangled in silver. She secured the matching blue sash around her tiny waist herself and stood pensively, hands on her hips, surveying the result.

"I can accompany myself on the pianoforte and I can play the harp and they both sound tolerably well if nobody listens too carefully. My singing voice is quite as good as many a young woman I have heard at Vauxhall Gardens and certainly better than any I have heard here at Frescati's, for to my mind the French cannot sing in key at all! But I am sure that none of these accomplishments are worth a jot unless I am also attractive to the men who pay to go there.''

Beatie paled visibly. "Sybella Howard—I will listen to no more of this talk.''

"Beatie, you don't understand. I am endeavouring to discover how best I can earn a living.''

Beatie squared her shoulders. "Let me see your tongue," she demanded.

"Nonsense! Really, Beatie, you are being most trying. If you would only allow me time to explain.''

"I am listening.''

"Very well then. I have been informed by Aunt Sophie that I am virtually penniless! In fact, without knowing it, I have apparently been dependent upon my cousin's benevolence for goodness knows how many years. That is the reason why Uncle Philippe has given his consent to Julian's proposal.''

Beatie studied her in silence for a moment. "I don't believe it," she murmured.

"Why not? Beatie, do you think she could be mistaken?''

"Mistaken—yes. She may also not be telling the truth.''

"Beatie, you must be wrong!''

"Yes." Beatie nodded her head and smiled humourlessly. "Yes, of course, I must be wrong.''

"Really, Beatie, you are being more than usually irritating." She waited until her feet were encased in the thin, heelless buskins of matching blue before she continued, this time with an air of finality. "At any rate, if it is true, then I must find work, and as there appears to be only two respectable positions open to a girl like myself—either a governess to some brood of odious small children or else companion to an equally objectionable old dowager—we must both endure the knowledge that I shall undeniably find it difficult to remain respectable." She finished smoothing her fingers into her long, white kid gloves and picked up her shawl of sequinned tulle. Beatie, not moving, stood purse-lipped beside her. With a sudden exclamation of exasperation, Sybella rounded on her. "Truly, Beatie," she declared, "anyone would imagine I was asking you to kick your heels at Vauxhall!"

The spontaneous gaiety of the French capital seemed to confute the past horrors of Revolution and war and to a girl of twenty, who had lived all her life in a small village in Kent and who had scarcely even tasted the pleasures of London's Mayfair, Paris was a city plucked straight from the pages of a fairy tale. It was to their credit that neither Sophie nor Philippe Servais had spared money in their attempts to entertain their niece during her stay and least of all in their arrangements for Sybella's farewell ball.

As she reached the top of the long, winding staircase that led down to the black and white checkered reception hall, Sybella caught her breath with excitement. Spangled stars, hung from the ceiling by uneven lengths of fine thread, formed a canopy from which a hundred shooting lights twinkled, captured by the flickering glow of the candles. Flowers and streamers festooned the staircase and walls, making the air heady with perfume. Through the open door of the house the wavering yellow lights of the lantern bearers moved to and fro in the garden as they waited the arrival of the guests, whilst in the ballroom, still hidden from Sybella's immediate view, the musicians began to play softly. The stage was set and over it all hung a mantle of rippling anticipation.

"Oh, it is all so beautiful!" Sybella's eyes shone as she turned to her waiting aunt and uncle. Sophie, resplendent in emerald green satin and a turban consisting of three very long purple ostrich plumes, nodded her head, well-pleased, not only by Sybella's compliment but also by her life in general which at this moment consisted of her gown, her musicians, and her love of parties. "Just think, this is my first ball!" Sybella went on. "Uncle Philippe, if nobody asks me to dance, you must swear to come to my aid!"

Her uncle's calm, grey eyes smiled good-humouredly. "I give my word." At the same time he opened her empty dance programme and made a note. "There, number twelve. By that time you will have captured the hearts of eleven good-looking young bucks and may, per-

13

haps, be a little tolerant towards a man of my mature years. Shall we proceed, ladies?'' He proferred both arms and with a flourish they slowly descended the staircase.

"I am certain this will be the most exciting night of my life,'' Sybella whispered. She could never have imagined that it was also destined to be her most fateful.

She saw him almost before he had entered the house. He was one of the last guests to arrive and he was standing in the doorway, his face half in shadow. He was very tall, the woman by his side scarcely even reached to his shoulder, and even though he was still so far away and she had no idea who he was or what he really looked like, she found herself being suddenly gayer and more vivacious, and she was aware that she wanted to impress him.

There were still four groups of new arrivals in front of him when she cast a further quick glance in his direction and found him gazing straight at her and in such a bold, almost impertinent manner that for an instant she was completely thrown off-balance. She looked away quickly, pretending not to have noticed, but although she fought the impulse with all her might, it was impossible not to steal just one more glance a minute or so later. This time he grinned and Sybella's mouth almost fell open in astonishment. How could he! she thought. But although she was morally positive that she should feel insulted, she was a little worried that her

14

only reaction was one of anger that he should have caught her.

She dragged her eyes away from him with a withering look that would have done justice to a woman twice her age, but though she fought to fasten her attention upon her guests, she could see only his face in front of her own and be painfully aware that every second was bringing their meeting nearer.

He was a man of about thirty-five years of age. His face was heavily tanned as though he had lived much of his life out of doors, his mouth strong and full-lipped beneath a thin, straight nose, his eyes dark and framed with lashes any woman would have envied. Yet for all his ruggedness his clothes were those of a dandy. His dark, curly hair was dressed in the latest mode of painstaking carelessness, and he even carried a gold quizzing glass between his slender, brown fingers. But there the similarity ended, and when he moved, there was an easy grace that unashamedly drew attention to the hard, lean, muscled body beneath the impeccably tailored suit.

Throughout the introductions Sybella faced him squarely. It was impossible not to feel flattered that a man so attractive should evince interest in her, but Sybella was also too young and inexperienced not to feel embarrassment and too unsure of herself not to imagine that perhaps it was simply due to the fact that her gown was unfashionable or her bodice too low.

Therefore, when the polite exchanges were over, she immediately feigned interest in her aunt's conversation with his companion, Madame Arlette Duval, one of Sophie's oldest friends. All the time she could feel his eyes on her, and her legs began to melt like jelly beneath her. At last she could endure it no longer and with an abrupt flare of defiance she turned to face him, her eyes coldly indifferent. Instead, he was smiling engagingly at Sophie.

"You will, of course, be our guest and stay overnight, Mr. Brady. The journey back to St. Dennis this evening would be far too tiring for Arlette. Besides I hear all sorts of disturbing stories of bandits. Only the other day I was told that a band of outlaws, former Royalists, no less, were captured after holding up a coach only five kilometres outside the gates!"

"You are most generous, both you and your husband, Madame Servais. Arlette and I gratefully accept your hospitality." His voice was warm and lazy and Sybella had the distinct impression that he was laughing at Sophie. But his face showed nothing but polite esteem.

Sophie fluttered coquettishly, obviously impressed, and she nudged Sybella playfully with her fan. "Did you realize Mr. Brady was English, my dear? Isn't that a pleasant coincidence?"

"Very pleasant, Aunt Sophie." Sybella kept her voice on an even keel.

"Isn't it, Miss Howard? But I have been thinking it strange we never encountered each other in London."

"Oh, I am afraid I have little to do with London society, Mr. Brady. My presentation was a very small affair."

"Then it is indeed society's loss, Miss Howard."

Sybella was certain his dark eyes were laughing at her now, and her voice took on an edge.

"But it is my gain, Mr. Brady. I much prefer the country to the city."

"How strange." His grin was tantalizing. "I am sure you will show me forbearance if I venture to change your mind?"

"Oh, I shall—but my fiancé, Lord Julian Rivers, might not."

There! She waited in triumph for the effect her rebuke would have upon him and a warm glow of satisfaction suffused her whole body. But with the merest smile of polite acceptance he bowed, turned to his companion, and without further ado they took their leave and strolled casually arm in arm into the ballroom.

"Now, what a charming man!" Sophie said. Her husband nodded his head in mechanical agreement but Sybella was too angry with herself for snubbing Adam Brady so effectively to even hear her.

As her uncle had predicted, Sybella had no difficulty whatsoever in attracting to her side every red-blooded young buck in the ballroom, and within ten minutes her programme had been completely filled. With her cheeks flushed with happiness and excitement she made a radiant figure as she flirted with her eyes and fluttered

17

her fan outrageously as if to the manner born. She was lovely, and if there had been occasions when she had questioned it in the past, she was now receiving ample proof of it and revelling unashamedly in the pleasure it was bringing her. Yet with each toss of her curls and ripple of laughter her eyes would dart to the one man in the room she wanted to impress most. Adam Brady. He was all she had been taught to distrust in a man, yet every other man there seemed a milksop by comparison. He had not attempted to speak to her again since their formal introduction and apart from his participation in a cotillion during the first part of the evening when for a few brief moments their hands had touched as temporary partners, she had not glimpsed him again on the dance floor. However, it was not until the dancing had stopped altogether for supper and Sybella was becoming hopelessly entangled with the most ardent of her young swains, that she lost sight of him altogether.

"You were saying, Marcel?" she murmured absently.

"I was saying I shall miss you most desperately, Miss Sybella. Say the word and I will go with you to London—to the end of the world if necessary!"

"Oh, my! Oh, no, you must not do that!" Sybella, only half attentive before, clutched his sleeve in sudden alarm.

He was a nice-looking boy with a riot of golden curls and such spaniel-like devotion in his brown eyes she had a momentary impulse to pat him gently on the head.

It was Uncle Philippe who broke in upon them with his bluff good humour.

"And how is our charming belle of the ball enjoying herself?" he asked.

"Oh, I am having the most wonderful time!" Sybella greeted his intrusion with thankful enthusiasm. At the same time, rashly deciding she could now afford to be just a little more generous to Marcel, she added: "How could it be otherwise with such handsome and attentive beaus?" Marcel's eyes shone with such a show of adoration Sybella felt a swift twinge of panic at what she had just done and with her brain whirling madly she clapped her hand to her lips and gasped: "Oh, but I almost forgot!" Without a moment's hesitation she rushed headlong into an explanation as she met the bemused expressions on the faces of both men. "Marcel, you must forgive me—I promised Uncle Philippe the very first dance after supper. Didn't I, Uncle Philippe?"

"Indeed, yes." His eyes twinkled as he watched his niece imploring him to answer her cry for help. "You wouldn't deny an old man such a small pleasure, eh, Marcel? Never fear," he squeezed the boy's arm, "you will have another chance later."

When they reached the balcony, Sybella subsided into a chair with a little cry of relief. "Oh, Uncle Philippe," she cried, "you were wonderful! But were you terribly shocked? Do you think I am quite shameless?''

"My dear child, you may find this difficult to believe but thirty years ago your Aunt Sophie fabricated a similar story. On that occasion I was also the fortunate man.''

"Do you think Marcel suspects?''

"Not for a moment. The hapless male is duped as always.''

"Now you are teasing me! But seriously, Uncle Philippe, I just had to get away from Marcel. I swear he would have asked me to elope with him within the hour!''

"Such a scandal,'' he joked, "and you the future Lady Rivers.''

"Oh, Uncle Philippe—please!'' All the ebullience died at his words. After a moment she shook her head. "I'm sorry.''

Her uncle regarded her not unkindly before he spoke. "I thought you were quite agreed on that subject, Sybella.'' She nodded and he went on softly. "You must realize this marriage is greatly to your advantage.''

"Yes.''

"Then it is settled in your mind?''

"Completely settled.''

"Good.'' He paused, uncertain. "Shall we go back inside?'' He joked, attempting to recall the easy relationship of a few moments back, "Perhaps I might claim that dance after all?''

"Do you mind if I stay here—just a little while by myself? It is so cool—I'd like to think—''

"Of course.'' He patted her hand gently and

moved to the entrance of the ballroom before he added quietly. "I'm very glad that you have made up your mind about Julian Rivers, my dear."

Even as she smiled at him, Sybella could feel the hot words bubbling up within her. She turned her back and took a long, deep breath, gazing sightlessly into the dark green shadows of the garden, in an effort to control herself, but to no avail. Like a sudden explosion it came.

"To Hell's fire with Julian Rivers! I swear I shall scream if I hear that man's name just once more!"

"That, my dear, is all this party needs to finish it once and for all!" The voice seemed to come from out of nowhere and Sybella stood transfixed, unable to open her mouth with mortification. "Though I'm not saying it would not be an original ending."

She felt her knees grow weak beneath her and she had to fight to retain the last few, but fast crumbling, shreds of dignity that she had left. That slow, lazy drawl—it was quite unmistakable. Then he raised himself from a chair that was hidden behind the shrubs that divided the balcony in two halves and he turned and faced her.

"How dare you!" she gasped.

"What have I done?" The handsome face wore a little-boy look of infuriating innocence.

"You—you listened! You heard everything!"

"I could hardly avoid doing so. After all, I was only sitting a yard away."

21

"You had no right!"

"I had every right. I arrived on this balcony first. It was you who intruded upon me."

"Mr. Brady," Sybella swallowed hard, "you are no gentleman!" The declaration seemed to come from the very depths of her being.

"In that observation I must admit you are not alone." He grinned cheerfully. "I have even been condemned to the same fate as your luckless fiancé. We appear to have something in common, don't we."

"You have nothing in common with my fiancé, Mr. Brady. I prefer that you did not speak of him."

"You know, Miss Howard, you are either the most inconsistent female I have ever encountered or you have an extraordinarily poor opinion of me."

If Sybella could have seen something to have hurled at Adam Brady at that moment, she would have done so. Instead, she turned imperiously on her heel and with his quiet chuckling ringing in her ears like the thunder from a thousand church bells, she swept across the balcony and into the ballroom.

The last guests took their leave shortly before one o'clock the next morning. There were three other houseguests besides Arlette Duval and Adam Brady, but they had already retired to their rooms, and the house seemed strangely silent after the festivities of the past few hours as the last carriage had finally lumbered its way down the drive and Sybella made her way upstairs.

The candles were softly burning as she opened the door of the room.

"Beatie, you shouldn't have stayed up," she chastised her fondly.

"And what else should I be doing?"

"Sleeping for one thing. We have to make an early start in the morning."

Beatie sniffed. "Don't you concern yourself over me. It's you who needs the sleep." She bustled about the room as she spoke, methodically packing away the garments Sybella was carelessly shedding into the almost ready luggage.

"Oh, I had such a wonderful night, Beatie!"

"Yes. Well I shall hear all about it tomorrow." She lit the night-lamp and placed it beside the bed. "Now you'll take a few drops of laudanum to make you sleep."

"Nonsense!" Sybella laughed away the suggestion. "Dear Beatie, you'd have trouble finding something to keep me awake!"

"Well—perhaps." She stood for a moment beside the bed, her blue eyes soft and very bright. Then she stooped and briskly brushed her lips across the smooth white forehead.

"Eight o'clock in the morning I shall be in to wake you!" And with that curt reminder she stalked out of the room.

Sybella snuggled luxuriously into the depths of the soft feather bed and waited for sleep to come. But the instant she closed her eyes, her

23

mind started slowly whirring. Over and over again the same pictures kept flashing before her eyes no matter how she strove to discipline them, and over and over she tossed and turned in her bed, pummelling her pillows until her wrist ached and growing more and more irritable with her own sensibilities as sleep became less and less likely to attain.

"Damn him!" she cried and she gave the top pillow a vicious blow. She had long since convinced herself that Adam Brady was probably the most despicable man she would ever encounter during her lifetime. She knew he was arrogant and conceited and that there was little chance that she would ever see him again and all of this should make her thankful. Instead, she was utterly miserable, for, unbelievable as it must seem, she had fallen—just a little—in love. That was the awful truth and she only fell eventually into restless slumber when she finally allowed herself to imagine herself being held in his arms.

It was still dark when she woke and she lay for some time savouring the guilty delights of a dream that still lurked in the corners of her mind. Then she frowned, suddenly conscious that something had disturbed her. She moved the candle-lamp closer to the clock to read the time. It was five minutes past three. Perhaps she had simply heard the hour of three. All around her the house seemed to be sleeping and with a little sigh she turned over and fell almost immediately asleep again herself.

The next time she woke, there was not the slightest mystery about the cause. Running footsteps were padding softly past her door combined with hoarse whispered voices that brought her bolt upright in her bed. Throwing aside the bedclothes, she swung her legs over the side of the bed and hastily lit another candle from the night-lamp. The instant she had done so she saw a darker shadow fall across the shooting shadows of the room.

She caught her breath and would have screamed had he not swiftly and efficiently placed his hand across her mouth.

"You do seem to be rather prone to screaming and I always seem to be preventing you." His tone was completely conversational. "But not just now—please, for my sake?" He removed his hand, listening carefully. Once again the house appeared to be silent.

"*You*!" Sybella gasped.

"Yes. But don't let us talk too loud."

She stared at him wild-eyed but there had been something in his voice, a simple sincerity when he had asked her to be quiet, that had removed any fear that she might have had of him.

"What are you doing here?"

"Hiding."

"*Hiding*! From what?"

"It is a very long and complicated story."

"That I can well imagine. I suppose you are a thief." She was astounded at the casual manner that she was accepting the situation. She studied him closely. He was completely dressed in a dark coat and breeches without a trace of colour. Even his shirt, if he was wearing one, had been hidden by the folding back of his coat lapel, so that in the shadows he was almost indistinguishable. She glanced at the small clock. It was only twenty minutes after three. "Well, this is my room, Mr. Brady, and I consider I am entitled to some explanation. Besides," she experienced a twinge of belated alarm, "what on earth would my uncle and aunt say if they found you here? Have you thought of that?" He didn't answer and she looked at the door with sudden apprehension.

"I locked it," she heard him murmur.

She turned her head slowly and he was looking at her. "What is it?" she whispered, her heart thudding.

"You are beautiful."

"I'm—you—" She closed her eyes. "You mustn't say—" She stopped short and her eyes grew round with horror. "Oh, my goodness! Oh, how *could* you!" With a frantic tug at the bed-clothes she had suddenly realized her appearance and clutching the bedspread she held it between trembling fingers against her chin.

"You are still beautiful."

"Tell me why you are here in my room or else I shall scream for help," she hissed at him.

"I am not a thief and my intrusion was quite unintentional." He paused and to her amazement she thought she detected a slight trace of
26

embarrassment in his manner. "I will be quite honest with you. I was visiting a lady." He cleared his throat. "A married lady whose name I would not like to see sullied by this incident. I was leaving by her—her window when I was seen by the dam' watch who thought I was a burglar and immediately raised the alarm. Very noteworthy of him," he frowned and it was all Sybella could do to restrain a smile, "but deucedly annoying! I am afraid your window was the only possible escape—temporary though it might be."

"No one saw you come in here?"

"Of course not. And I hope no one sees me leave!"

"Thank you. Dare I ask if my honour is as precious as that of your lady friend?"

"Every bit—I promise." His voice was completely sincere.

"Well—well—it is quiet now. Don't you think you had better try?"

He nodded and moving to the windows, gingerly opened the curtains. "Blast!" The exclamation so soft Sybella saw only his lips move. She looked at him questioningly. "They are searching the garden."

"What then—" She did not finish. "S-s-h." She held up her hand. "They are coming back. What if they want to search the rooms? Where can you hide?"

He was already beside the window once more. "They have gone," he whispered

"Are you certain?" Her voice betrayed more concern than she had intended and she felt her face grow red.

For just one moment the surprisingly boyish grin was there on his face. "Goodnight—and thank you," he whispered. "I'll repay the kindness." Then he was gone.

"Sybella!" It was Sophie's voice. "Are you all right?" The doorknob rattled impatiently.

"Yes, Aunt Sophie." She leapt out of bed and ran and unlocked the door.

"Oh, my dear, such a fuss!" Quite out of breath, her lace nightcap askew, Sophie was distractedly fanning herself with its flowing ribbons. In the background Sybella could see her uncle with two or three servants bearing candles.

"What has happened?"

"Not a thing—not *one* thing!" She threw a stormy glance in her husband's direction. "For months I have been telling your uncle that the watch was far too old to ever see anything. Well, now he has started seeing things that don't exist!"

"What did he see?" Sybella murmured.

"He believed he saw an intruder. It is so dark outside this evening I doubt whether I could have seen anybody myself—and my sight is perfect!" She patted her hand absently. "Go back to sleep, my dear. It is still early." She swung around on her husband. "Come along, Philippe! Send the servants back to bed and come to bed yourself! Oh dear, now here comes Beatrice. Well, I'm afraid you'll have to deal with her yourself, child. I just know that if I don't return to my chambers this instant, I shall have to call for the hartshorn." With an exhausted sigh she promptly departed, surprisingly quickly, in the direction of her room, followed at a suitable distance by Uncle Philippe and the servants.

Sybella drew Beatie into the room when they had gone. "Please, Beatie, I must have something to make me sleep."

Beatie nodded her head dolefully. "I should think you will need something—all of us for that matter. Though what we shall be closing our eyes to the good Lord Himself only knows! Praise be to Him that we are leaving here today, for not one more night would I spend under this roof!" All the time she was complaining, she was uncorking the laudanum and carefully measuring the dose. "To think that for three weeks we have been at the mercy of a watch who is almost blind and practically deaf! We could have both been murdered in our beds! Now, get back into bed and take this." Sybella made a face and swallowed the mixture but Beatie paid no attention to her familiar plea for a piece of sugar to remove the vile taste, as she always did. Instead, she crossed to the window. "God save us!" she exclaimed. "The window is open! Simply asking for trouble. Imagine if someone had tried to enter."

"But nobody did, Beatie."

"I know that, but the watch imagined he saw a man leaving through this window."

Sybella frowned. She watched Beatie carefully lock the windows and draw the curtains before she spoke.

"Did the watch say that? I thought Aunt Sophie told me he was seen to *enter* through my window." She punctuated the lie with a careless little laugh.

"Well, she was wrong—not that it matters a jot. I spoke to the watch myself. He told me the intruder came out of this window and he even pointed it out to me. Immediately afterwards he raised the alarm. Of course, the poor wretch is so blind he could not even see me properly at first although I was standing right next to him. He thought I was the butler!"

Sybella swallowed a smile. Nevertheless, she told herself, the much maligned old man was not as blind as everyone imagined although he was wrong about the window. She shrugged her shoulders under the bedclothes. What did it all matter? Even Adam Brady himself was probably asleep by now.

The rush of the following morning, the farewells, Sophie's inevitable tears, then her own tears as Sophie handed her the most beautiful shot-silk sunshade she had ever seen in all her life as a going-away present—all of this combined to drive the excitement of the previous evening out of her mind. It was therefore not until she and Beatie were in the carriage and well on their journey to Amiens, their first stop, before she began to think of it again.

Lulled by the swaying rhythm of the carriage,

the warmth of the day, and the soft snores that came from Beatie, Sybella closed her eyes and allowed her thoughts to wander. Of course the watch must have made the simple error of imagining Adam Brady was leaving her room when actually he was seeing him enter it. But no, that was wrong. The alarm had already been given before that could have happened. Adam had told her so himself. Besides, that was the reason why he had used her room to hide in. She frowned, no longer drowzy, and opened her eyes. Something at the back of her mind kept hammering away, insisting there was more to remember. Something she had forgotten. Like a nagging tooth it kept on and on until at last it stopped—and she remembered.

Three o'clock. She had awoken at three o'clock and had experienced the sensation of having been disturbed. That was nearly twenty minutes before the alarm had been given. No! She dismissed the thought as ridiculous—and yet it still persisted. But that could only mean that Adam Brady had been in her room for twenty minutes before the alarm. And if so—*why*?

Chapter Two

"Oh, fiddle!" Sybella shook herself angrily.
Why, she was behaving like a ninny! It was
most unlikely there could be anything more to
Adam Brady's nocturnal visit, scandalous as it
was, than what he himself had already told her,
and it was high time she put a stop to her own
fertile imagination that was hoodwinking her
into believing otherwise. There! she told herself. Now let that be the end of it!

Pretty as a picture in a walking dress and
bonnet of pale green, a jade green travelling
cloak around her shoulders, she sank back once
more against the soft, ruby velvet upholstery of
the smart, new crested carriage belonging to her
aunt and uncle that was taking her to Calais.
She glanced at Beatie, snoring away softly on
the seat opposite her, and she smiled gently.
The roads were bad and, well-sprung though the

32

carriage was, it jolted and jarred constantly, and Beatie's bonnet, which had been slipping gradually for some time, now rested roguishly over one eye. Yet, despite her rakish appearance, even in slumber Beatie Crewe wore an air of unbending disapproval.

The day was warm and very still, the late summer sky a bright azure blue with just a thin smudge of white brushed lightly along the horizon. From the window of the carriage Sybella stared out at the fast-moving countryside, green and peaceful and disturbed only by the peal of a cowbell or the squawk of a bird, alarmed by the approaching horses. It seemed that nothing on earth could ever shatter its tranquility until, suddenly, the charred remains of a desecrated church or the ruined walls of a once proud castle, nakedly silhouetted against the sky, would smote the eye and give a pitiful reminder of The Terror that had so recently purged the land.

A hundred yards away, a lone horseman, his cloak billowing out behind him, appeared from out of nowhere and galloped swiftly past the carriage. An expert rider herself, Sybella watched him admiringly as he disappeared beyond the slight rise just ahead of them and she wondered idly how well Adam Brady could handle a horse. It seemed perfectly natural that he should enter her thoughts so easily. She had never met anyone like him in her life before. Nor had she ever dreamed that a man could bestir such vastly contrasting emotions after such a brief acquaintance. She was sensible enough to realize that most of those emotions were those of an impressionable and inexperienced girl, but there was something else that worried her. She had found men attractive before but they had invariably been youths of her own age and none had possessed a fraction of the attraction she had found in Adam Brady. His was a raw, almost blatant, virility that seemed barely to rest beneath the surface of his lean, tough body. It was challenging and demanding and, what was more, it frightened her.

A particularly nasty bump started the carriage aseesawing and Beatie's bonnet left her entirely. Sybella waited until they had both regained their composure before she spoke. Her green eyes sparkled mischievously.

"Did you sleep well, Beatie, dear?"

"*Sleep!*" She sniffed loudly and jammed her grey bonnet back on to her head with rather more than necessary vigour. "I'd like to know how a body could dare to close its eyes and never be sure it would open them again? Why, the entire countryside is riddled with highwaymen and marauding bands of emigrés. I couldn't sleep a wink." She fixed Sybella with a baleful eye. "If I closed my eyes, it was just to say a prayer."

"Then we should be most favoured, Beatie, dear."

"I should feel more so if we had a man along with us for protection."

"We have Jean-Louis. He has been Uncle Philippe's coachman for nearly thirty years. Why,

34

he knows this road like the back of his hand.''

Beatie tied her lips into a tiny knot of dissension. "We have an old man to see us safely out of one country and a small boy to see us into the next!"

Sybella laughed outright. "Cousin Ronald is as old as I am and I am sure he is quite capable of protecting us."

"I trust Providence will agree with you," she retorted dryly. But it was quite clear she did not believe it would.

Their journey had been well planned and night was barely closing in when the carriage reached the outskirts of Amiens and proceeded directly to the Tête de Boeuf where it had been arranged for them to spend the first night of their three-day journey to the coast. A blast on the horn from Pierre, Jean-Louis' ten-year-old groom, alerted the innkeeper, and before Jean-Louis had entered the cobbled courtyard, the ostlers and postboys were already waiting for them.

Spurred on by a reward that seemed certain would attend a new and expensive-looking vehicle carrying two British ladies, the courtyard became a scene of almost overwhelming zeal as the horses were unhitched and led away and the small mountain of trunks, portmanteaus, and bandboxes unloaded from the top of the carriage, all within minutes of the carriage steps being laid down and the two passengers being safely deposited at the door of the inn.

The proprietor himself was a slight, wiry figure in ill-fitting black silk breeches that bore the

35

unmistakable traces of moth repellent and his welcome was as determinedly enthusiastic and every bit as exhausting as his ostlers.

"A thousand welcomes, my ladies!" He bowed from the waist, executing a generous flourish with his right hand as he did so. In the other hand he held firmly a small lighted lantern. Your chambers have been prepared and are awaiting you."

"You are most civil, monsieur," Sybella acknowledged his greeting with a smile.

"Henri." He bowed once more.

Beatie, who had been listening to these exchanges and, at the same time, surveying their surroundings with a growing melancholy, now intervened with her usual crisp directness. "Tell us, Henri," she demanded, "can we be sure that this sorry sight will not collapse upon our heads during the night?"

For a moment the buoyant jollity came dangerously close to sinking. Then he smiled affably. "You may be sure,"he promised her politely.

Built in a semicircle around the courtyard, the building had been badly damaged during the war and the left wing was merely a tangled wreck of charred and twisted timber. Seen against the flaring torchlight that illuminated the yard, it appeared both ghostly and depressing. The wing they were now entering was badly pitted but the interior was warm and surprisingly cheerful and through an open doorway came the appetizing smell of good country cooking.

A scrubbed brick floor, uneven with the years, led through on the right to a beamed dining room. Directly ahead of them stood the staircase leading to the bedrooms. The place appeared spotlessly clean and where the walls were not heavily panelled they had only recently been carefully whitewashed.

"You must have suffered a great deal during the war," Sybella remarked, anxious to make amends.

"It was not pleasant." He shrugged his shoulders fatalistically. "But I was fortunate it was not worse; I was left with half an inn. Now the war is over and the happy times will come once more." He started up the stairs, still carrying the lantern, and they followed. "Already many of your countrymen have stayed the night at my inn this summer. Soon there will be sufficient money to commence building."

"Have you any other visitors staying here at present?"

"No." The reply came so swiftly and abruptly Sybella was forced to turn and regard him with surprise, but he smiled instantly and added, "You are my only guests at the moment." He stopped outside the first door on the left of the stairs and turned the handle.

"This is your room, m'am'selle," he told Sybella. "Hot water has been ordered and will shortly be brought to you. In the meantime, if you would care to partake of a little wine and biscuits," he indicated the refreshments laid out on a small table by the window, "I shall make

37

arrangements for supper.'' He hesitated uncertainly. ''You will dine downstairs?''

''Thank you.''

He bowed and withdrew but Sybella waited until Beatie had been shown to the adjoining room before she closed her own door and took stock of her surroundings.

A central light of only four candles gave a very mediocre glow to the room, small though it was. However, like the rest of the inn it was clean but sparsely furnished. There was no panelling and the walls had been freshly whitewashed. A brightly woven patchwork quilt was spread cheerfully across the huge four-poster bed and crisp, white curtains, tied with red ribbons, nicely framed the latticed windows.

Sybella threw off her bonnet and cloak and crossed over to the table. She glanced through the window and could just make out the grotesque shadows of the ruined wing. She shivered, although she was not cold, and turned quickly away. The inn was depressing and she wished Jean-Louis had not stopped at it, but from all accounts it was the only suitable lodging in Amiens and it would have been quite out of the question to have travelled on farther at night. She poured herself a little of the wine and, nibbling at a biscuit, took the glass with her to the bed and sat down. The wine was raw and she choked on her first swallow but by the time she had finished the glass she felt much better. A few moments later her luggage arrived. It was still being brought in when two small boys staggered into the room carrying a tub between them that was quite large enough to have held them both, whilst behind them came a third boy and a girl, each carrying buckets of hot water. She went to her purse and counted out four livres and handed it to the eldest boy. The expression on his face was so rewarding she wished the light had been better to see it and even made her forget the fact that the time was fast approaching when she would have to count every farthing.

Bathed and refreshed, Sybella was dressed for supper when Beatie came to collect her three quarters of an hour later. Even she appeared to have mellowed somewhat.

"Well, child," she asked, "shall we proceed to the dining room?"

"Why Beatie, you old fraud—I do believe you have been drinking!"

"You believe well, my dear. An uncommonly good wine, even if I do say so. We must ask Jean-Louis to procure some from that nasty little man to take with us."

"I think you are being unfair to Henri. He is rather sweet. Besides, I feel sorry for him."

"I don't. I think he is a thimblerigger," she gave a little chuckle at her own skittishness, and added, "but shifty eyes have never ruined a pot of broth so let us see what awaits us for supper."

There were seven other tables in the dining room, all empty but all with fresh linen. Henri himself attended their table, bringing in the first course of steaming onion soup. The main course was a stew, served from an enormous copper pot. There was possibly a great deal more vegetable than meet in it but it was deliciously cooked and much thought had obviously gone into its preparation.

Sybella was halfway through her meal when she put down her fork with a little shiver and glanced behind her.

"Are you feeling chill, child?"

"A little. I believe a draught is coming from the front door."

Beatie pushed back her chair. "I'll fetch your cashmere."

"Be still, I can get it myself. I know precisely where it is packed." With a little smile she left the room and crossed lightly to the staircase.

"M'am'selle?"

His appearance was so sudden and unexpected she gave an involuntary start. Then she laughed. "You startled me, Henri."

"Did I, m'am'selle? Forgive me."

"Of course." She attempted to pass but he stood directly in her path at the foot of the stairs. "Excuse me, please, Henri."

Ignoring her request, he asked, instead, with apparent concern, "Is supper not to your liking?"

"It is very enjoyable."

"M'am'selle will be returning to the dining room then?"

"Yes." Sybella frowned, puzzled.

"Perhaps then if m'am'selle told me what she needs, I could get it for her?" He seemed as embarrassed now as Sybella herself was. His face burned a dull red and she noticed that the hand resting on the balustrade, so casually barring her way, was trembling.

"No!" Her suspicions were now thoroughly aroused, though for what reason she did not attempt to fathom, and without further hesitation she thrust him to one side and ran headlong up the stairs. With the advantage of having surprise on her side, Sybella had caught the innkeeper off-balance and he had staggered and almost fallen to the floor. But when she looked back at the top of the stairs, he had disappeared.

Puzzled, hardly knowing what she was doing or why, Sybella stole silently to her bedroom door. Only when she stopped to listen outside did she realize the extent of her agitation. Her heart was pounding so wildly she could hear nothing else and her head was swimming sickeningly. She forced herself to take a deep breath in a desperate attempt to pull herself together. She was being quite absurd, she told herself. Why, it was most likely her ridiculous imagination was at work again. Crimson flooded into her face as the possibility took root in her mind. What if Henri was simply being over-attentive? Why, he would think she was a lunatic! He would think she was drunk! Perhaps she was! She put her fingers to her lips as the laugh started to bubble up inside her and then she suddenly stiffened, listening. She waited. Without a second's delay she flung open the door.

The poor light in the room made it difficult at first for her to realize exactly what was happening. She saw the shadow of the intruder crouched upon the floor and felt rather than saw him leap to his feet and throw himself past her into the passage. Before she could even open her mouth to scream, she had been pushed heavily back against the door. It was all over within a matter of seconds, yet when she stumbled to her feet the inn was completely silent and there was no indication to even say where the intruder had darted.

She hesitated by the door, uncertain what to do, realizing that even if she called for help there would be none coming from Henri or anyone else at the Tête de Boeuf. She moved into the room and stared down at the floor. Every piece of luggage was open. But strangely, there was no disorder. She frowned and fell on her knees beside her belongings. She made a rapid search of each bag. Nothing seemed to have been taken. There was nothing of value to take, of course, she told herself. But a thief could only know that afterwards. She stared at the luggage blankly. The only possible explanation was that the thief, with Henri's cooperation, had imagined he had plenty of time to systematically go through every piece of luggage. Why, if she had not decided to go to her room during supper, she would most probably never have even known that her luggage had been rifled. So this was how the Tête de Boeuf intended to rebuild its left wing! Her legs felt suddenly very weak and she crossed to the small table and poured herself a glass of wine. When she had finished it, she sat down on the side of the bed and tried to think. She knew it would have been quite impossible for her to describe her intruder. It was all so quick, so unexpected. She could not recall if he was dark or fair or whether he had been wearing a hat, but, paradoxically, she was certain of one thing, she would know if she ever saw him again.

That night Sybella moved all her belongings into Beatie's room and the two women slept together, each clutching the other. They left the inn at seven o'clock the next morning, an hour earlier than planned, and when Sybella presented the money to pay their account, she was informed that Henri offered his regrets and apologized that he had had to go to market. It was not until they had been travelling for well on an hour that either woman began to relax once more.

They travelled all that day and reached Montreuil at sundown where they stayed the night, leaving again at nine o'clock the following morning with ample time to reach Calais.

The town clock had just chimed the half hour of three when Jean-Louis drove their carriage through the gates of the town. Ahead of them stretched the long, narrow harbour of Calais, the blue water sparkling beneath the rays of the warm afternoon sun, and the instant Sybella poked her head out of the carriage window and looked around her, her fatigue vanished as if by magic.

"Beatie, we are here at last!"

"Indeed we are and not a second too soon. What's more, I pray we remain no longer than we must."

"Oh, fiddle! Now promise you will not be a misery, Beatie. We have one whole hour before the packet sails to enjoy ourselves."

The carriage had at that moment entered the marketplace and it suddenly seemed that the whole world had started talking at once. Women in red camlet jackets and high white aprons, long lappets flying from their caps, stood at open stalls shouting their wares, fish their menfolk had only just caught, fruit and vegetables and gaily painted eggs. Wooden sabots and horse's hooves clattered on the cobbles. Disenchanted ladies stood hopefully in open doorways, their eyes on hightobys, naked to the waist, golden rings in their ears, mingling with the English tourists and scissoring their way through countless unsuspecting pockets, disappearing seconds later with their own bulging. But Sybella saw only the glamour and she drank it all in with shining eyes.

She jumped down from the carriage the moment it stopped, not even bothering to lower the steps, an engaging sight in her gown and bonnet of yellow muslin. She opened the modish shot-silk sunshade Sophie had given her and twirled it impatiently between her fingers, the cynosure of many a male eye as she waited for Beatie to descend.

"Do hurry, Beatie."

"Where are the steps? Would you have me break a leg?"

"Heaven forbid!" Sybella slammed down the steps with a weary sigh but good-humour was not far distant from her eyes as she helped her old abigail to the ground. Beatie's acid comments and complaining ways had been part of her life for far too long for her to be really put out by them. Besides, they were rarely of any account and both of them knew it.

After instructing Jean-Louis to proceed to the wharf with their luggage, they joined the milling throng, but they had been wandering for less than ten minutes when they were overtaken by Pierre. He tugged at the hem of Sybella's skirt with timid fingers.

"What is it, Pierre?"

His thin little face was all eyes but never more so than when he smiled, which he did now. "Follow me, please," he bade them importantly and, still grinning, he disappeared into the crowd, leaving the two women to follow as best they could. Minutes later they arrived breathless at the passenger office to find Jean-Louis waiting for them.

"There is no boat." He spread his hands helplessly.

"Nonsense!" Beatie pushed forward. "There it is in the wharf."

He shook his head and pointed to the chalked

notice scrawled above the closed ticket office in front of which a small group of bewildered passengers like themselves were gathered.

"Parfait Union—crossing cancelled. Next sailing 0900 hrs," Sybella read the notice aloud and turned to Beatie in dismay. Most of her high spirits at seeing Calais had been engendered by the knowledge that within five hours they would be in Dover, for, although she would never have admitted it and would have undoubtedly pooh-poohed any similar admission from Beatie, the events of the past few days had unnerved her sufficiently to have no desire to spend another night unescorted in France.

"Why, this means we shall have to arrange accommodation at a hotel." She stamped her foot. "Why has it been cancelled?" she demanded irritably. "They offer no explanation."

"It is the weather, I'm afraid, ladies. Deucedly annoying, isn't it?"

The voice was quite unmistakable. Deep and lazy and just that faintest tinge of insolence. Sybella felt the warm colour surge into her cheeks and she spun her head to look up into the laughing face of Adam Brady.

"My compliments to Miss Howard and Miss Crewe." He bowed perfunctorily.

Even though his image had been so much in her thoughts these past few days, Sybella's heart still skipped a beat and she decided he was even better looking than she had given him credit for. He was hatless. A superfine navy blue box coat of many capes was draped casually across his broad shoulders, and his towering height seemed even greater now in the shining, military-style top boots, the height of Parisian fashion, that he was wearing. She allowed her eyes to linger just that fraction of a second longer than she knew she ought, and when her eyes met his once more, she was instantly aware that he had noticed. She blushed anew and spun her parasol disdainfully.

"I must say I fail to find anything wrong with the weather, Mr. Brady. In fact, I think it is delightful." She glanced significantly at the blue of the sky that extended across the channel as far as the eye could see. "I should think there is some mechanical fault, Mr. Brady. Probably a compass," she added grandly.

"A commendable reason not to sail, Miss Howard. However, I think, perhaps, you have overlooked the wind in this case."

"There isn't any wind," she snapped.

"Exactly. We are becalmed. Now that is the crux of our problem as a sailing packet must have wind for the sails."

Now he really was laughing at her and out loud too. With the utmost difficulty she swallowed her angry rejoinder as being too unladylike and managed a frosty smile in return.

"Now," he continued, "may I be of assistance to you two ladies?"

"I think not."

"Indeed, you may!" Beatie made the correction in an instant. "Perhaps you would be good enough to recommend a hotel for us to stay at, Mr. Brady."

"Of course. I suggest Dessein's. Miss Crewe, if you ask your driver to collect your luggage and drive you there in your carriage, Miss Howard and myself will follow in mine. If you should arrive first, just give your requirements to the hotel clerk, but be sure to mention my name."

Before Sybella could offer any protest, he had taken her firmly by the elbow and was already guiding her towards the waiting curricle. She swept her eyes admiringly over the pair of matched greys before she spoke. "It is indeed very kind of you, Mr. Brady, but I could make the necessary arrangements at the hotel you mentioned."

He assisted her to mount into the curricle. "I doubt that, Miss Howard, but as I am returning to Dessein's in any case, it is of no accord."

"Are you staying there also?"

"Of course. It is the best hotel in Calais and, I may add, extremely full now that the packet is not sailing. I doubt very much that you would be able to arrange accommodation without my name."

Really! Sybella ground her teeth until they ached. Why, it wasn't her imagination. The man was truly insufferable! She wanted to make a stinging retort and could think of nothing quickly enough. When she had, it was too late as he had already changed the subject.

"Do you drive, Miss Howard?" he asked as he was about to take the reins.

"Of course," she assured him scornfully.

"Then perhaps you would care to exercise these greys. I think you might find them to your liking." Dexterously changing seats, he handed her the reins and then sat back with an air of detached politeness.

"Which direction should I take?" she asked casually, smoothing her yellow gloves over her wrists, her heart thumping wildly.

"You can take this road directly ahead of us and skirt the town. You should be able to get in a pretty dash before we must get back into traffic once more."

"Thank you." She gripped the reins and swallowed hard to steady her nerves. Julian owned a pair of greys as fine as these but he had always forbidden her to drive them and it had been a long time since she had handled anything so well matched. Nevertheless she was determined she would die before she would disgrace herself as she was sure he expected her to.

The greys were restive and they plunged forward the instant she gave them their heads. She almost gasped but schooled her lips into a smile just in time. She had not gone more than two hundred yards before she felt confidence returning to her. The greys were well trained and easier to manage than she had suspected. Besides, she was suddenly aware of Adam Brady's admiring sidelong glances, though he said nothing. Dragging off her bonnet, she shook out her curls and sat back, enjoying herself mightily. It was not until she had finally drawn the curricle to a halt outside Dessein's that he spoke.

"If you learn to exercise a stronger right wrist, Miss Howard, you could make a quite passable driver."

Her eyes glittered but she rallied sufficiently to reply coolly: "Thank you, Mr. Brady. If only I could acquire you as my tutor."

The lobby was noisy and crowded and Beatie was waiting for them as they entered. A "House Full" sign was propped on the counter beside a bored-looking clerk. Sybella glanced from the sign to Beatie's face. "You could not get accommodation?" she asked, not with a certain relish.

"I did when I mentioned Mr. Brady's name."

Sybella smiled wanly. "Well, thank you very much, Mr. Brady," her tone was brisk, "Now, if you don't mind, I think we should like to retire to our rooms."

"Of course. I shall make arrangements for dinner. Will eight o'clock be suitable?"

"I believe I shall dine in my room, Mr. Brady. I'm an old woman with weary bones and you are just being polite anyway. However Miss Sybella will join you, I'm sure. Goodnight, Mr. Brady."

"Now why did you say that?" Sybella demanded furiously when they were out of earshot. "You know I shan't be there?"

50

"Really? You surprise me, child." Beatie's blue eyes sparkled in her sour face.

"You surely don't think I am interested in Mr. Brady?"

"Oh, of course not." They reached their room and Beatie sniffed. "After all, it wouldn't do much good if you were, would it."

Sybella waited until all their luggage was in the room before she commented. "Why wouldn't it?" she asked.

Beatie carried on as if there had never been a pause of more than five minutes in the conversation.

"A man of thirty-five, or thereabouts, child, who is as attractive as Mr. Brady and remains single must put a great deal of effort into staying that way. It will take a remarkable young woman to pry him loose, mark my words."

"And a mighty desperate one!" Sybella finished tartly. Nevertheless, she spent the next hour wrecking her packing searching for the correct accessories to her silver satin dinner gown.

Dessein's Hotel was traditional in design, built on a cobbled yard on three sides. It was well cared for and expensive and Sybella was soon to discover that it not only boasted a theatre within its walls where comic opera and the straight drama was performed by well-known artists from the principal theatres of Europe, but it also offered a cuisine comparable with any in Paris. It was here that Adam had reserved a table.

"Is it to your liking?" he asked her as she sat down.

They were in a secluded position of the dining room beside an open window opening out into a sculptured garden. Orange and acacia trees had been illuminated with coloured lamps that lent a soft lustre to the green leaves. In the distance could be heard the faint ripple of water on pebbles.

"It is delightful."

"I'm glad."

She felt his eyes on her and broke the silence that was threatening to embarrass her. "May I ask what you are doing in Calais, Mr. Brady? Are you returning to England? I had no idea you were leaving Paris."

"Nor I, Miss Howard." He grinned. "It was, you might say, an impulsive decision."

"Oh dear, no trouble, I hope. You did mention," she went on as he raised his eyebrows questioningly, "that the lady with the neighbouring window had a husband, I fancy."

He chuckled. It was nice to see the laughter lines net his eyes. Then he inclined his head. "Touché," he murmured.

Adam Brady proved himself to be a gay and charming companion when he cared to make the attempt, and before many moments had passed, Sybella was completely at ease and even enjoying herself.

"When do you think we shall sail?" she asked.

"Nine o'clock in the morning as scheduled, I

52

should think. A breeze will no doubt spring up later this evening." He paused. "Are you in such a rush to return to England?"

"Now that my holiday is over, I shall be glad to return," she confessed.

"It surely can't be that you are anxious to see your fiancé?"

Julian! Sybella's heart sank as she realized that for the past hour Adam Brady had quite succeeded in dismissing the nagging problem of Julian Rivers completely from her mind. She frowned, silently preoccupied with her own thoughts, and Adam raised his eyebrows in gentle admonition.

"Surely you still remember him?" A smile played about his mouth. "The poor fellow you publicly disavowed."

"I—didn't—I—*really*! Mr. Brady, you take our cordial relationship too much for granted!" She searched frantically for the right words, all the time aware that he was merely needling her yet unable to resist swallowing his bait. "I did no such thing," she gasped at last, "and even if I did, it is unthinkable of you to mention it. After all, you *were* eavesdropping!" She took a deep breath, determined to wipe away the laughter lines she could see creeping around his eyes. "Besides I *am* marrying Julian Rivers."

"Well, I'm glad to hear that. I never like to see a lover's spat go on too long."

"It was not—" Sybella checked herself. "I must ask you not to discuss the subject further, Mr. Brady."

"As you wish, Miss Howard."

They spent the remainder of the meal on relatively safe ground but Sybella soon discovered it was quite impossible to remain angry with Adam Brady for more than a short time. She also discovered, to her pleasure, that he was a warm and friendly person beneath the shell of cynicism he wore and an amusing and well-informed companion.

Her eyes sparkled as he related an amusing anecdote concerning a debt he owed a certain female proprietor of an exclusive St. James's gaming house.

"Unfortunately I chose an evening when I was short of ready cash and she was on a winning stake. I went down to her in four out of five rubbers of picquet and lost two hundred and fifty guineas." He smiled reminiscently. "I was very young and, well," he cleared his throat, "shall we say, for the purposes of this story, that I owed her considerably more than a mere gambling debt, so when she asked me to grant her a favour, I could do nothing except accept. She told me my debt would be paid if I merely spent the next four weeks telling everyone I knew that I had never won so much money nor seen such well-run tables than at her establishment. Well, I agreed and she told me later that the increase in her business after that night was substantial. But it cost me far more than two hundred and fifty guineas. Why, I had every shark and fair-weather friend in London hanging onto my coattails for a good six months afterwards!''

They both laughed together.

"You must be very well known, Mr. Brady.'' She hesitated. "Are you a professional gambler?''

He threw back his head and laughed loudly. "No, I'm not. Now, does that disappoint you?''

"No, I'm glad.''

He regarded her quickly and then smiled. "I have a mother who lives in Cheshire. I live there with her three months of the year and pride myself that I run the estate for her—which of course I don't. She has a far better head for business than I have and she is even a better picquet player, but we fool each other into believing otherwise. Apart from that we are very fond of each other. You must meet her one day. You would like her.''

For a moment there was more in his voice than the words conveyed and Sybella blushed self-consciously. She lowered her eyes and was relieved when the waiter came to their table to take away a few remaining dishes.

The tolling of a bell caused her to look at Adam in surprise.

"It means it is ten o'clock and every person out on the streets must be furnished with a light. It is the law.''

Sybella clapped her hands together with pleasure. "Can we go out into the street?''

"Of course.''

55

The gates of the hotel were closed and they had to wake the porter. Grumbling throughout, he found them each a lantern and lighting them, handed them over.

"What happens if they go out?" she whispered to Adam.

"We shall be thrown into jail."

"To see Beatie's face, it might even be worth it!"

The night was pitch black and Sybella gasped as they reached the street. "Why, it is like fairyland!" And indeed it was. Hundreds of lights, of all shapes and sizes, flashed continuously, rising and falling, remaining stationary, fast and slow. For all the world like giant, fat fireflies.

A man passed without a lantern and Sybella turned to Adam anxiously. "Will he be caught? Perhaps he doesn't know."

Adam smiled at her concern. "He has a pipe in his mouth. As long as it is alight, he isn't breaking the law."

"You're joking!"

"No, that is the law also. The glow doesn't have to come solely from a lantern." Sybella digested this statement in silence and Adam chuckled. "Ladies are naturally excluded. Now, would you care to stroll down to the waterfront, Miss Howard?"

"I think that would be very pleasant, Mr. Brady."

They could see the Parfait Union tied up at the wharf, waiting for the morning. Already a slight breeze was stirring the harbour.

"What are you thinking about?" Sybella broke the silence softly.

"I'm thinking that England is just the other side of that little strip of water."

"It isn't far, is it."

"It is too far for Napoleon Bonaparte, Miss Howard."

Sybella frowned. "Why do you talk like that? You said things like that at my party."

"So I did."

He offered no other explanation and Sybella pursued the subject a trifle irritably. "You think there will be another war, don't you, Mr. Brady?"

"Miss Howard, I still don't agree that this one has ended."

"Oh, fiddle! I don't wish to discuss such things. I think we had better return now to the hotel, Mr. Brady. It must be getting late."

She offered him her hand as they reached the door of her hotel room. "Thank you for a very pleasant evening, Mr. Brady." She smiled shyly. "I really did enjoy myself."

"I too, Miss Howard."

Sybella hesitated, her hand on the knob. "Shall I see you in the morning?"

"Of course. I will make all arrangements for your luggage."

"Oh—I did not mean that! Besides, Jean-Louis will look after our comforts until we sail."

"I understand, Miss Howard, but it is my pleasure." He bowed. "I trust you will rest well." With a slight inclination of his head he smiled and turned on his heel.

Sybella turned the handle of her door and her heart was singing. The room was ablaze with light but she scarcely noticed the fact, her head was too full of absurd but delicious notions. Consequently she was totally unprepared for anything like the sight that was about to greet her.

"*Satan's oven!*—" She caught her breath in one long, horrified gasp and for an instant all she could do was stand rooted in the doorway, praying her legs would continue to support her, unable to trust them to take her forward or back. Then with a strangled sob she flung herself down onto the floor beside the inert figure in the centre of the room.

"Beatie! Oh, Beatie, darling, what has happened!" But Beatie was quite incapable of explaining. Trussed up like a bag of old clothes, she had been gagged, blindfolded, and bound hand and foot, and apart from one rather unnerving moan that seemed to promise that it would flower into fuller expression later, there was nothing to reassure an almost hysterical young girl. Cascading from open drawers, on chairs and both beds and all over the floor was strewn the upturned contents of all their luggage.

Her throat dry with anxiety, Sybella tore at the gag and blindfold with trembling fingers. This time Beatie's moan was loud and telling and her expression when the gag was removed

58

was encouragingly murderous.

"Oh, thank God!" Sybella breathed. "What happened? Who was it?"

"I knew it would happen! I told you, remember? I said we'd be murdered and I was almost right! We are in a heathen land. We're doomed!"

"Did you see the man?"

"*Man*! My dear child, I was set upon by an *army*!" She rolled her eyes with frustration. "I saw nothing. The cowards attacked me from the rear!"

All the time Sybella was tugging at the cords that bound Beatie's wrists and she was unaware of the movement behind her until she felt the strength of the fingers on her shoulder.

"*Adam*!" Relief and strain together combined to bring the tears to her eyes and in her distress she never even noticed that she had used his Christian name.

"I thought I heard you cry out—I wasn't certain." He was already on his knees beside her, freeing Beatie from her cords, chafing her hands between his own.

"Oh, she looks so pale!" I'll find the ammonia and water.

Beatie sighed weakly. "Brandy," she corrected.

"She will be all right," Adam assured her. Sweeping one of the beds clear of clothing, he returned to Beatie and lifting her into his arms like a child, deposited her gently between the sheets. She responded with a beatific smile, finished the remainder of her brandy in one swallow, and instantly went to sleep.

Adam chuckled softly to himself before turning his attention to Sybella.

"Don't worry," he told her gently.

"But I *am* worried."

"We will go through your belongings together and discover what has been stolen. I will notify the manager."

"You don't understand. This isn't the first time. And I'm certain nothing will have been stolen!"

"Why do you say that?" He studied her thoughtfully.

"It's true—I know it. The same thing happened to our luggage at Amiens two nights ago. But why? I have no jewellery except the little I wear. There is nothing else of value except my clothing."

For a while he seemed as puzzled as she. Then he shrugged his shoulders and tried to laugh. "Perhaps you have something precious and you don't even know about it! What about all those presents you are taking back? Your gift for Julian for instance."

Sybella was so distracted she even missed this gentle barb. "No, you're wrong. I have no gifts for anybody—not even for myself except that sunshade my aunt gave me." She pointed to the door where it hung.

Adam nodded, his eyes lingering on the dainty item, then he pressed his hand firmly over hers. "These are unhappy times for France despite what they tell you to the contrary in Paris. The people are poor, many of them desperate, and I fear you have been doubly unfortunate. This has been a very unpleasant experience, but I do wish you would now try to dismiss it. Do not allow it to ruin your wonderful holiday.''

Sybella Howard, although she might never have noticed it, had changed ever so subtly since the evening of her farewell ball such a short space of time ago. There was a bloom about her now that had never been evident then. She seemed suddenly to have become a woman, and it had brought with it not only all the doubts and problems she had always imagined would be miraculously left behind but a string of new ones as well. She closed her eyes and endeavoured to sleep but again and again it was Adam Brady who forced her back to wakefulness. She thought of his words of reassurance. He was so kind and tender when he desired. She chewed her bottom lip thoughtfully. He was right—she must forget. But why, the question gnawed, if the thieves had been so desperately needy had they not stolen a few of her clothes, at least, to keep themselves warm?

The Parfait Union sailed as scheduled at nine o'clock the following morning. Adam Brady was as good as his word, attending to their every need throughout the four-hour voyage. Shortly after they sighted Dover, he begged to be excused, explaining that he wished to supervise the landing of his carriage and horses and it was not until they were landing that she saw him once more briefly.

"Sybella! Sybella! Here I am!" The young man with the shock of red hair gesturing excitedly from the wharf was Ronald Rivers. As different from his brother Julian as it was possible to be, his boyish face with its freckled snub nose was, at his moment—as at most moments, slit almost from ear to ear by an irresistibly lopsided grin. Three months younger than Sybella he was noisy both in manner and attire and his canary yellow waistcoat and elaborately knotted purple cravat was causing noticeable attention, even on this grey, drizzly afternoon, when combined with coat and breeches of a more than brilliant burgundy.

"Ronnie!" Sybella's face lit with pleasure. "Do you see him, Beatie?"

"Brilliantly," Beatie murmured dryly.

"He does not seem to have changed at all. He is still the same harum-scarum Ronnie, I do believe." She waved back happily.

Five minutes later the Parfait Union was tied up and the gangplank laid down. For a few seconds she glimpsed Adam Brady on the deck and then he was lost once more in the rush to disembark. Hiding her disappointment, she hurried down the gangway and into Ronnie's waiting arms.

Except for one or two brief visits during the summer holidays, it had been all of two years since Sybella had seen her cousin. They had grown up together, played together, and got into trouble together. Ronnie had even declared

62

his undying love at eleven and had impressed Sybella considerably by stabbing his thumb with a nail in a grandiose attempt at corroboration. This had resulted in a poisoned hand and a box on the ear from Beatie but for months Sybella dreamed of the time when he would fight duels on her behalf.

He held her at arm's length. "Let me look at you. Why, you are beautiful! What happened?"

"Odious boy! I've always been beautiful but you were too full of yourself to notice!"

"And Beatie! You look younger than ever!"

Beatie sniffed. "Well I don't feel it!"

"Beatie had rather a harrowing experience last night," Sybella put in quickly. "We shall tell you all about it afterwards."

"Did she indeed! And what about my experience? Do you realize I arrived here twenty-four hours ago to meet this packet and last evening I had to sleep on the sofa in the foyer of the Ship Inn because there was not a room to be obtained in Dover? I am aching in every joint."

"I can see that you and Beatie are going to have a lot in common." Her eyes were on the gangplank and she moved forward quickly as Adam Brady disembarked. For a minute or two they conversed. Then, lifting his hat to her and to Beatie, he moved on.

"Who was that fellow?" Ronnie's eyes followed him admiringly.

"I'm sorry, Ronnie, he was in a hurry, otherwise I would have introduced you." She glanced at Beatie. "He is a friend of Aunt Sophie's. We

63

met him by chance last evening and he was kind enough to assist us to find accommodation.''

"Big chap. Splendid cravat.'' His face suddenly broke open again. "Quickly, we are getting damp standing around. I've made arrangements for the luggage to follow on. Jason is waiting outside with our carriage."

"They had been travelling for less than thirty minutes during which time Ronnie had scarcely stopped chattering. He longed to go to Paris himself and he assured them, or himself, that now he had finally left Eton with honour—there had been five threatened rustications during his turbulent career there—Julian would allow it. Sybella had been aware that there was another carriage close behind for some minutes. Now the horse's hooves were very close indeed and from the sound of it they were travelling at a tremendous pace. She was about to comment upon it to Ronnie when she was suddenly flung sideways in her seat and almost hurled through the door as their carriage swung crazily off the road, missing a tree by inches.

Ronnie leapt from the carriage onto the road, shaking his fist with indignation at the back of the fast vanishing vehicle. "Why, whoever was driving must be a maniac! We could have all been killed!" He turned to Sybella who had joined him and his face was crimson. He turned his attention to their driver. "How is it, Jason? Is there much damage?"

"One wheel has separated from the wood,

sir. I'll have to get a smith. I'll take one of the horses, sir, if that's all right."

Ronnie kicked the offending wheel with his foot. "Fudge! This is going to delay us for hours unless we can find another carriage! Oh, well," the grin returned, "now you can tell me all about Paris."

Sybella tried hard to match Ronnie's gaiety, but time and time again she found her mind wandering and Ronnie asking her questions she had not heard, and she was startled to discover how tensely she was sitting and how taut were her nerves. *But she had seen them! She was certain of it!* The overtaking carriage had been travelling at top speed and it would have been impossible to identify the occupants but she was almost certain of one thing. *The carriage had been drawn by a pair of perfectly matched greys!*

Chapter Three

Rivers House had been home to Sybella for as long as she could remember and she knew and loved every inch of the thickly wooded grounds in which it stood, isolated from its nearest neighbour by nearly five miles. Built during the first half of the eighteenth century, the house itself was Early Renaissance in design with Dutch trimmings, the latter, a most fashionable innovation of the period, being displayed in the three stepped gables. The result was a singularly clumsy marriage between two different styles that had been mercifully tempered down the years by the large-leafed ivy that now practically covered its hard red brick façade.

Sybella had grown to look forward to that first warm surge of well-being swept over her whenever she first glimpsed the house again after an absence. But now, for the first time in her life, as the carriage swung into the drive and she saw the friendly bank of chimneys silhouetted against the sky, that feeling was missing and in its place there was unease.

The carriage was about twenty yards from the house when the huge oak front door suddenly opened and a pool of golden light went spilling out into the night. Seconds later the tall, thin figure of Julian Rivers emerged, followed closely by a liveried servant bearing a lantern. Together the two men waited for the carriage to draw even and finally come to a halt.

"Greetings, brother!" Ronnie jumped down from the carriage with his customary verve, a blinding grin on his face and an itch for tomfoolery. With great panache he assisted Sybella to descend and led her at arm's length to Julian's side.

"At excessive risk to wind and limb, I hereby deliver one undamaged beauty." He winked at Beatie and added, "Plus one slightly worn old dragon."

"And a mere twenty-four hours overdue. Praiseworthy, indeed, my dear Ronald." Even when he tried, Julian's voice never seemed to quite match his smile.

"It wasn't Ronnie's fault, Julian," Sybella protested mildly. "The channel was becalmed. The packet did not sail until yesterday morning."

"I know, my dear. I read the notice in this morning's edition of the *Post*. But I am glad you are here, nevertheless." He bent and kissed her affectionately on both cheeks, at the same time relieving her of her reticule and the sunshade she was holding. "You look lovely, Sybella, though a trifle tired. Did you have a pleasant trip?"

Ronnie, who was helping Beatie down the carriage steps at that moment, chortled loudly. "You ought to ask Beatie, brother dear. I am certain she will give you a graphic account of it if you do. Wouldn't you, Beatie?"

"Indeed I will! Though after what I have been through, I should immediately take to my bed!"

Julian turned sharply. "What happened?"

"Nothing of significance, Julian." Sybella broke in swiftly and glowered at Ronnie. She felt sufficiently depressed not to welcome yet another of Beatie's turgid recitals. "We shall relate you all our gossip presently. In the meantime I believe I should like to warm myself."

Julian seemed about to say something, then apparently thinking better of it he paused just long enough to murmur a few instructions regarding the luggage before following her quickly into the house.

"Stay here and warm yourself before the fire." He strode the length of the hall to a door at the rear. "I'll inform Mrs. Fallon you have arrived."

The room they had entered was large and heavily beamed and filled with treasures that had passed through many generations of the Rivers family. The superb oaken staircase and huge stone fireplace set directly opposite it shared pride of place, but only for a moment, and then

68

one became aware of the rich carpeting, the heavy brocade at the windows, the finely tooled furniture, and the paintings that hung from the panelled walls. Sybella believed some of the splendour came directly from her family, but she had no more dreamed of questioning ownership than she had of questioning her position in Rivers House. Only now, in the last few days, had she realized that in a few brief months time when she came of age she would be no more than a guest in this house. Unless, of course, she married Julian.

She had removed her cloak and bonnet and was standing in front of the fireplace, staring down into the flames, deep in thought, when the woman entered.

"Welcome back, Miss Sybella." The voice was cool and polite and quite impersonal.

Sybella started and turned. "Oh, Mrs. Fallon! How nice. Thank you." She started to make a friendly move forward then stopped, colouring a little, as the housekeeper turned slightly away to flick at an imaginary speck of dust with her apron.

Barbara Fallon had been the housekeeper at Rivers House for a little more than a year. Quietly spoken and even quieter in dress, she was an attractive brunette who was still only in her early thirties. Sybella knew she had come with impeccable references through a highly respectable employment agency when old Mrs. Fox, her predecessor for more than forty years, had finally been pensioned off by Julian. But who she was and where she came from and even if she was a widow, Sybella had never been told. Barbara Fallon had never offered confidences nor had she asked for any and she seemed perfectly content to continue in this manner.

"I hope you had a pleasant holiday."

"Thank you, I did."

"I am glad. While you were away, I took the opportunity of having your room freshly painted. I hope you will be pleased with it."

Sybella, who hated her belongings being turned upside down when she was not there to supervise it and who was quite certain Barbara Fallon knew it, set her mouth in a pleasant smile.

"I am sure I shall, Mrs. Fallon," she murmured.

"Cook has some roast beef in the kitchen if that will be all right. I am afraid none of us knew when you would arrive exactly."

Before Sybella had a chance to answer, Ronnie had burst into the house.

"Roast beef? A double helping please, Mrs. Fallon. I've a most famous appetite after that journey."

Barbara Fallon nodded her head quietly and glanced at Sybella once again.

"Thank you, Mrs. Fallon. Tell cook just a small portion."

"And what about Miss Crewe?"

"Food? I could not swallow a spoonful!" Beatie declared witheringly, her critical gaze riveted on the luggage until it reached the staircase. Then, as she followed the servant upstairs, added, "But I shall force myself."

Without further word Barbara Fallon withdrew.

Ronnie made a face as she closed the door leading to the kitchen.

"You know, Sybella, if I am going to live in this house once more, something has got to be done about that woman."

She answered his brilliant grin with a slight smile. "What did you have in mind? Poison?"

"Go on! You're bamming! Not a bad idea though." He chuckled.

Sybella raised her eyes to heaven. "Good Lord, I believe you mean it!"

"What about a sudden epidemic of mice? I believe that worked very well on Mrs. Pringle. Or was it Tingle?"

"Her name was Dingle! And the cook who replaced her was far worse than she was. Do you remember that also?"

"Oh yes. That was rather unfortunate." He brightened. "But that is no reflection on our mice. It was simply Julian's lack of judgment." He smiled. "It shows he hasn't improved in ten years doesn't it."

Sybella laughed. "You really are a lamb, Ronnie."

"I know."

"And conceited!" She paused, before asking in a different voice. "How long will you be staying, Ronnie?"

"Until I'm thrown out."

"No—please tell me."

71

"About six months. Julian has made me promise I will live here until I come of age though I would dearly love a place in London. But I can't do that without funds and Julian isn't forthcoming. Don't see why I have to wait. It's my money and six months can't make all that difference. Julian can be uncommon mean about a few guineas when he has a mind to it." He paused to regard her thoughtfully for a moment. "What is it, Sybie?" he asked gently. "Is something wrong? I've noticed you were jumpy but I thought it was because of those two upsets you had in France. It's more than that though, isn't it? Do you want to tell me about it?"

Sybella kissed him lightly on the cheek. "Do not worry about me, Ronnie. I'll be all right."

"Well, don't forget Cousin Ronnie if you want to unload any troubles. He cannot cope very well with his own but he is wizard at looking after other people's. Ask Julian."

"Ask Julian what?" Julian entered the room briskly. His voice was almost gay and he appeared to be in such unusually high spirits Sybella could scarcely take her eyes from his face.

"I was saying we should ask you to open a bottle of wine to celebrate Sybella's homecoming."

"An excellent idea. We shall do just that. You've already made arrangements for supper?"

"Yes, Julian." Sybella swallowed her annoyance. She had hoped she might have had supper in her room instead of which, Ronnie, bless him, had turned the meal into a party. "I'd like

72

to change my dress, if you'd excuse me." She gathered together her cloak and bonnet. "Oh— my reticule—"

"I sent it upstairs with your luggage, my dear. Also your sunshade."

"Thank you, Julian. I shall hurry."

"Do not bother. I shall still be here when you come down."

They ate in the small, panelled dining room reserved for the family meals and Mrs. Fallon presided over the serving of it. To Sybella the meal seemed interminable although Julian retained his good humour and Ronnie appeared to enjoy himself immensely—mainly by baiting Barbara Fallon at every possible opportunity. But if she noticed, it did not seem to vex her. Though on more than one occasion Sybella had the feeling that Julian was on the verge of intervening. Nevertheless, the meal finished without any unpleasantness and Sybella drew a sigh of relief.

Immediately it was over, Ronnie got up and settled himself in front of the fire. After a great deal of leg stretching and throat clearing, he cast a speculative glance at Julian. Watching him from the table, Sybella found it so easy to guess his intentions and she closed her eyes and prayed that he would not allow himself to be tormented by his brother. She knew them both so well. Ronnie could be so painfully eager and Julian was ever willing to allow him his head— but so often as a cat would a sparrow. Finally,

73

after he had given the fire a quite unnecessary and almost fatal jab with the poker, he spoke.

"I've been thinking, Julian, that I would like to go into the village tomorrow if you do not mind. I saw a pair of those York tan driving gloves and Miller has a famous selection of new spurs in stock." He swallowed hard. "You know, they say it is quite the high kick of fashion in London to wear a single fancy spur."

"Is that so?—"

"Yes—er, so they say. Er—I thought perhaps I might take the new bay. I mean—if I may." Ronnie rushed on breathlessly. "I mean I *can* handle her, Julian, and I would dearly love to ride her in. She gave me no trouble the other day."

"No, I saw you the other day. I was most impressed. Very good indeed." A muscle twitched in Julian's jaw.

Ronnie's eyes widened with eagerness. "Really, Julian? You really were impressed?"

"Yes, that's what I said. Now I suggest you go and get a good night's sleep."

"Yes, you're right!" He jumped to his feet and made for the door. "Well, thank you, Julian. Er—coming, Sybella?"

"No, Sybella and I have a great deal to talk about yet." His thin lips parted in a smile as he glanced across at Sybella. "Goodnight, Ronald."

Ronnie hesitated at the door. "It is all right, isn't it?"

"About going to the village? Of course."

"Well—I really meant—it is all right about the bay?"

"Oh! I'll think about that, Ronald. She had a great deal of exercise today. Ask me again in the morning."

For a moment Ronnie's blue eyes sparked. Then he controlled himself with a languid shrug of his shoulder.

"Well, I suppose I can always take the black," he said, closing the door quickly behind him.

Sybella waited until she heard his footsteps hurry away before she looked at Julian. He was smiling quietly.

"Let him take the bay, Julian. Tell him so tonight before you retire. Will you?"

"Is it so important?"

"It is to Ronnie."

"And to you?"

"Perhaps."

"Very well then. I shall tell him." He stood up and drew her over to the fireside. "You have a gentle heart, Sybella dear. A most endearing quality." He patted her hand possessively. "Now, let us talk about more important things than Ronald's excursion to the village." He smiled. "A wedding, for instance."

Sybella marvelled at her own feeling of calm. This was the moment she had dreaded yet now it had arrived she felt nothing except relief that it would soon be over. She allowed him to take her hands and hold them tightly between his own.

75

"You will marry me, won't you, Sybella?" he asked her earnestly. "I wish it so very much."

"Yes, Julian. I will." The words came easier than she had ever dreamed would be possible.

He relaxed instantly. "Thank you, my dear. You have just made me a very, very happy man indeed." He sprang to his feet. "Come! We must drink to this! Why, it is an occasion in a man's life when the woman he asks to marry accepts!"

Watching him as he poured out the wine, Sybella could not help being a trifle flattered by his obvious pleasure at her acceptance. His thin, high-boned face was flushed and a fine layer of perspiration clung to his upper lip. He filled her glass and handed it to her. Then, taking his own, he said simply: "To our future, my dear." He rolled the wine around on his tongue, savouring it before swallowing. Picking up the bottle, he returned with it to the fire.

"I should like to have the banns read before the end of this month if that is agreeable to you, my dear."

Sybella started involuntarily. "So soon?" she whispered.

"Whyever not? Why should we wait? After all, I am your legal guardian and your aunt and uncle, who are your closest relatives and whom I thought it courteous to ask, were most enthusiastic."

"But there are so many arrangements—" she faltered, "my wedding gown—I must go to London—"

"All arrangements will be speedily made, have no fear on that score. As for your wedding gown and your personal requirements I shall have Bond Street, Mayfair, come to Rivers House. Never forget, Sybella, your position. You will quickly learn that people will be only too eager to serve Lady Rivers at *her* pleasure." He chuckled at her silence. "You will soon get used to it, I assure you. Come now, let me refill your glass."

"No, I really shouldn't, thank you, Julian." She attempted to match his gaiety. "I am afraid I shall get tipsy."

"Nonsense. You will sleep deeply. Nothing more." He hummed a tune as he refilled both glasses. For a moment he chuckled to himself as if he were enjoying some private joke and then he turned to Sybella, his glass in his outstretched hand. "My dear," he said with a slight thickness, "I suggest we propose a toast to your dear Aunt Sophie. Let us drink to a truly remarkable woman!"

It was well past midnight when Sybella finally retired to her room. As she opened the door, she glimpsed Beatie in the soft light sitting in the straight-back chair beside the bed, snoring softly. She closed the door behind her and crept in softly. "Beatie, dear." She touched the old woman's hand gently. "You should be in bed," she scolded her as she opened her eyes. "I can look after myself."

Beatie sucked in her sunken cheeks still further and made typical sounds of dubiety with her tongue. "As long as I am alive I shall look after you. Now get undressed. The warming pan is in the bed, though it is so late I should think the coals are long cold." She eyed Sybella shrewdly as she unbuttoned her dress. "While we are on the subject of warming pans," she murmured, "has he asked you to marry him?"

"Yes, Beatie." Sybella turned and faced her old abigail squarely. "But I will not marry him," she declared quietly.

"But you told him you would?"

"Yes."

"How long have we got?"

"A month—no more. Oh, Beatie, I am so frightened now. I am not at all certain that I could go and earn a living. In fact I am not at all certain what I could do."

"Do not be frightened, my darling. Beatie will help you. And you have done right. You have gained time so that we may plan what is to be done."

During the crisp, autumn days that followed Sybella's return from France, there was a decided change in the atmosphere of Rivers House. On the surface there was a bustling, exhilarating air of activity as plans for the forthcoming wedding were put into effect. From early in the morning until late at night there seemed to be a constant stream of vehicles in the carriageway and Julian seemed to be actually enjoying the divertissement. Sybella escaped whenever it was possible and for hours she would go horseback riding in the brilliantly tinted Kent countryside surrounding the house, drinking in her stolen hours of freedom until eventually she forced herself to return once more to the house. But beneath this hive of activity there was a growing tension that was made even more deadly by virtue of its concealment.

The relationship between Julian and Ronnie had always been a difficult one, a major factor being the great disparity in their ages and Julian's natural position of authority. Ronnie's years at Eton had partially removed the strain from Rivers House although a score of five threatened rustications during this period had scarcely engendered tranquility at either establishment. However, since his return their relationship had deteriorated further, on Ronnie's part it had virtually flared into open revolt, and scarcely an evening passed without some clash between them. Even so, Julian's extraordinarily maintained good humour continued to manifest itself. Then, two weeks after Sybella's return from France, this mood changed abruptly.

Some nights later Sybella and Ronnie chanced to meet in the passageway outside their bedrooms when Sybella opened her door just as Ronnie was leaving his room.

"Why, Ronnie!" Surprise and pleasure were mingled in her greeting.

"Cousin Sybella!" He wagged his finger at her playfully. "Little girls shouldn't spy through keyholes! Don't you know that?"

Sybella flushed and snapped crossly. "I know

it is the only way to be certain of seeing you any more!" She put her hand on his and drew him into her bedroom and closed the door. "I want to speak to you."

"Not now, Sybella." He turned to depart, a youthful but dashing figure in his long-tailed coat of blue cloth and fashionable pale yellow breeches and top boots.

"*Now*, Ronnie." He turned, resignedly, and waited whilst Sybella regarded him with troubled eyes. "You are going into the village again tonight?" she asked gently.

"Of course."

"Ronnie, stay at home."

"I have an engagement."

"You could break it?"

"No I couldn't."

"Then have dinner with us first. Why, I don't believe you have eaten at home more than three or four times since I came back from Paris. I feel quite upset."

She was trying desperately to make her voice sound light but she was failing dismally and she knew it and she also knew that Ronnie was regarding her with growing impatience. Finally he could restrain himself no longer.

"Oh, Sybie! What are you doing to yourself!" She did not reply and he carried on with mounting exasperation. "Why are you marrying Julian? Why? What does it all mean? You are unhappy and it is so obvious I cannot understand why Julian himself does not see it also." He paused. "Maybe he does, I am prepared to believe anything of my charming brother. But *you*! You don't love him. I would not believe it if you told me. So why? Has he some sort of hold over you? No, that is impossible. Then what is it? Sybie, *tell* me! Let me help you.''

Sybella was close to tears but she still did not speak. Ronnie studied her carefully for a moment, the faint, bluish-tinged smudges beneath the wide-set green eyes, the paleness in her face that was accentuated by the black mass of her hair, and he shook his head sadly. "Very well, I shall mind my own business.''

"Ronnie," she shook her head, "don't worry about me.''

"Do you know what you are doing?''

"Yes.''

"I am glad." He put his hand on the door-knob but he paused with her next question.

"Ronnie, will you be gambling again tonight?''

"What of it?''

"Ronnie, please stop hitting out at him. You are only hurting yourself. Why can't you wait just a few more months until you come of age? Try and live here in harmony until then. I know he would be different if you tried.''

"Try?" He laughed bitterly. "Do you have any idea how many times I have tried? Of course you haven't. Do you realize he will not even give me a shilling unless I go down on my bended knees?''

"Ronnie, he will not honour many more of your gambling debts.''

"No one is asking him to. My creditors all

81

know I inherit my share when I am twenty-one. They are willing to wait until then." He placed his arm around her waist and kissed her gently on the cheek. "Thanks for being concerned, Syb," he whispered before opening the door. He paused on the threshold and turned back, the old, familiar grin suddenly splitting his face. "By the way," he said, "I met a friend of yours last evening." He went on jauntily. "He made me assure him on my honour that I would convey to you his kindest regards."

"Really? I am sure I cannot think who he might be." She smiled. "Stop teasing and tell me who it was."

"Adam Brady."

"Adam—!" Her mind fled back to the journey home from Dover and her cheeks coloured. Of course she had been wrong about the overtaking vehicle belonging to him. She frowned. There was so much concerning Adam Brady that required explanation and yet the very mention of his name was sufficient to turn her legs to water and wipe all questions from her mind!

"Yes," Ronnie went on. "You recall that big chap? Wore a splendid cravat."

"What is he doing in this neighbourhood?"

"He is lodging at the Horse's Head, G'night!"

So near! He was so near! Why, she thought with a swift surge of her old confidence, it was only a matter of time now before Adam Brady would be presenting his visiting card at the front door of Rivers House.

Ever since their first meeting Sybella had

82

been unable to erase either his face or his voice from her thoughts, although it must be admitted that all attempts had been noticeably halfhearted. She had longed to see him again and she had scarcely ever dared to hope that she would. Now, here he was only a few miles from her and he had even conveyed already his kindest regards. Why, surely this was sufficient proof that he, too, had thought about her! This last speculation arrived so unexpectedly and proved so devastating Sybella almost fainted on the spot out of sheer exultation and promptly decided to go at once into the village herself. However, feminine logic prevailed before she had time to order the carriage and she told herself that such a move would undoubtedly make her appear far too interested. Instead, to occupy her time, she spent the waiting hours planning and replanning the wardrobe she would eventually wear when they met. But the days dragged past and nothing happened.

Then, just as she felt she could bear the uncertainty not a moment longer, the strange sequence of events that had been so cunningly entangling her in its pattern these past weeks, now chose to weave, a little more, its unsuspected web about her. It began with Ronnie. He knocked on her bedroom door one morning while she was dressing for breakfast.

"Ronnie, how very nice!" This time surprise and pleasure were truly blended in Sybella's greeting, but Ronnie's first words instantly wiped the happiness from her face.

"I have come to say good-bye," he told her simply.

She looked at him with dismay. "Not now. Not today."

"Yes, Sybie. We had the devil's own argument last night. I felt certain the whole household must have heard it. Anyway, I made up my mind I would get out today. Julian can play the Grand Panjandrum with somebody else from now on."

"I suppose it was over your gambling?" Her voice was miserable.

"I dropped another hundred pounds. Julian found out."

"*Oh, Ronnie!*"

"Now For God's sake don't start preaching to me, Syb. It's over. I'm going. I realize now I should never have come back home."

"Does Julian know you are leaving?"

"Not yet."

"Then don't do anything yet. Let me speak to Julian. I feel sure he will listen to me. I can smooth matters over, Ronnie, I know I can."

"No, Sybie." He stopped her gently. "You don't understand. I want to go."

"But *where*?"

"I shall stay at the Horse's Head until I can get myself a place in London."

"But have you sufficient money? I could give you a little but all I have is not—"

"Thank you, Sybie," Ronnie broke in. "I can manage on what I have for a time. Besides, I am entitled to an allowance from Julian and I shall ask him for it." He paused, his face suddenly more grave than Sybella had ever remembered it but his next words took her completely by surprise. "Come with me," he whispered. "Pack your belongings and leave now. Don't go through with this marriage, Sybie."

"Ronnie—I—I couldn't go now—not at this moment—I—I just couldn't!" The words spilled from her lips in a flurry of confusion.

He nodded his head understandingly. "Well, I believe I had better go now. Jason is waiting for me. Take care of yourself, Sybie." He kissed her gently on both cheeks and Sybella watched him cross to the door and leave the room without another word.

Ronnie's unexpected departure from Rivers House proved to be the added stimulus needed for Sybella to arrive at a decision regarding her own immediate future. She had never at any time intended to go through with the marriage to Julian although without the intervention of a miracle she had no idea how she intended to accomplish it. For a time she had dreamed that Adam Brady might provide that miracle but as day followed day it had become increasingly obvious that this would not be so. With a sense of shame Sybella realized she had simply never faced the reality of her position and that there was only one avenue open to her. Consequently she made up her mind to face Julian and request that he release her from her promise. She hoped that, as her guardian, he would not order her out of the house until her twenty-first birthday and by then she would have made her plans how to live. Immediately the decision had been reached, the tension of the past weeks seemed to fall away like magic and in its place she felt an upward surge of excitement. Why, she told herself angrily, she surely had been mooning her days away like some poor little downstairs maid! Sleep, which had seemed difficult enough to court five minutes before, was now quite out of the question. Flinging back the bedclothes, she jumped out of bed and, without further reflection, put on her robe and slippers and left the room.

It was Julian's habit to remain in his study until midnight and Sybella ran lightly down the darkened staircase to the hall below. As she reached the bottom step, a sudden chill made her draw her thin robe closer around her and she noticed with quick surprise that the roaring log fire was nearly dead, the candles almost gutted. Frowning a little apprehensively, she moved slowly towards the grandfather clock standing to the left of the staircase and, peering at its face, was astonished to see that it was already twenty minutes after twelve o'clock. Crestfallen, she was about to turn back to the staircase when a sudden impulse made her change her mind and she crossed instead to the short, narrow corridor that divided Julian's study from the drawing room.

She was still two or three yards away from

the study door when muted sounds of conversation from within started to filter through into the corridor, bringing her abruptly to a halt. Sybella had never really expected to find Julian still downstairs. Thus she was doubly surprised when she not only discovered that indeed he was but that there was also someone with him.

She hesitated uncertainly, her own purpose for being there momentarily forgotten. Little more than an hour ago she had said goodnight to Julian outside this door and he had made no mention of expecting a midnight caller. She frowned perplexedly. A caller at this late hour must surely be bringing only a message of extreme urgency and her thoughts immediately flew to Ronnie. Was her headstrong young cousin already involved in some serious trouble? Impelled by curiosity, she moved forward, bending her head to the door just as Julian stopped speaking. For what seemed to be an interminable span of time she remained crouched in this one position and the silence within the study continued to grow until she was forced to move away from the door lest the thudding of her own heartbeat betray her presence. Then, just as the impossible notion began to haunt her that perhaps Julian had actually been talking to himself, his visitor started speaking.

At first Sybella could hardly believe her ears and she told herself she was wrong, that there was merely superficial resemblance to the voice that she knew so well. But though the tone was

87

no longer quiet and dispassionate, she knew, beyond all question, that the voice belonged to Barbara Fallon.

"I didn't mean to say those things—I swear I didn't! But you have no right to treat me like this."

Sybella listened incredulously and then the frightening coldness that she had heard so often in Julian's voice cut through the short silence that followed this outburst.

"Really? I had no idea there was a book of etiquette that dealt with these matters, my dear. Perhaps you could enlighten me? Should I supply you with an itemised invoice for services rendered for instance? You could add your own figures later."

"Stop it, Julian! I beg you!"

"And I beg you to be silent! I have no mind to appear heartless but the whole situation is fast becoming maudlin and absurd and quite unnecessarily tiresome. You have always known the extent of our relationship and you have accepted it. As far as I am concerned that relationship can continue but the decision is entirely yours."

There was again a long pause and Sybella waited, her whole body by this time aching with cold and cramp. The grandfather clock in the hall began to chime the half hour and she sprang away from the door fearful that she would not hear the warning footsteps should either Julian or Mrs. Fallon go to the door. When it had finished chiming, Julian was replying to something Barbara Fallon had just finished saying and his voice was heavy with irritability.

"I have no intention of changing anything, Barbara. The business with the girl is my affair. Your threats are stupid and wearying. I bid you goodnight."

Sybella waited no longer. She turned and ran blindly back through the silent, darkened house to the familiar security of her own room, and only when the door was closed behind her did the painful, sobbing gasps of tension at last begin to leave her.

It was very near dawn before Sybella finally fell into a heavy, dream-laden sleep only to be awakened some time later by a movement beside her bed. With a strangled scream she hit out into the dim light, flinging herself violently away from the hands that sought her.

"Sybella! Child!" Sybella heard her name as if it had come through many layers of wadding. The next instant she was wide awake and Beatie was standing over her.

"It's you!"

"Of course it is me!"

Beatie's familiar tone of tart reproval acted upon Sybella like a welcome douche of cold water and with a little gurgle of laughter that was almost all relief, she put out her hand and gently touched her arm.

"Beatie, dear, I am so sorry. I must have been having a nightmare. Did I hurt you?"

"A little stimulant may relieve the pain."

"You know the whereabouts of the brandy

bottle better than I, Beatie. You don't need me to give it to you." She started to laugh again and then, suddenly, the night and all its forbidding disclosures came back to her with a rush.

"What time is it?" she asked quietly.

"Half past eight." Beatie eyed her shrewdly as she opened the curtains and coaxed in the pale, early winter light. "Did you sleep well?"

Sybella looked at her guardedly. "No—not very well."

"Neither did I." She opened the wardrobe drawer and began selecting fresh underwear. "Neither did a number of people," she murmured off-handedly.

Sybella waited impatiently for Beatie to elaborate further but she was concentrating upon the contents of the wardrobe with infuriating diligence.

"Beatie, what *are* you hinting at?" she demanded finally.

Beatie shrugged. "Maybe I imagine things."

"Did you hear anything?"

"Indeed I did."

"What? Tell me! Beatie—I am *not* wearing that cerise dress so you can put it straight back on the hanger!"

"You said last night you wanted your cerise."

"I don't care what I said last night! But just be *still!* Now, tell me what happened!"

"You don't think I was foolhardy enough to go walking around this house in the middle of the night, do you?"

90

"Beatie, you are being deliberately evasive."

"Well, I'm hiding nought that you won't find out for yourself the moment you get downstairs."

"Do you think you could bear to give me the news yourself?"

Beatie sniffed. "She's gone! Our little bird has vanished in the night."

"Who has gone?" But immediately she asked, Sybella knew the answer.

"Mrs. Fallon. Jason drove her into the village so that she could catch the early morning stage to London. And good riddance, too! Although I daresay I shall be expected to do her work now as well as my own."

Sybella nodded her head, her mind in a whirl. "I believe I shall wear my cerise today, Beatie dear," she murmured absently.

Weary though she was, Sybella faced the new day with more fortitude than she had dared to hope she could muster. She no longer felt the slightest respect for Julian and with this barrier removed she felt no longer any guilt in her decision to break their engagement. However he failed to put in an appearance for breakfast and she was forced, once more, to bide her time.

Julian's morning appearances tended to be erratic as it had always been strictly observed by the household that no one, not even his personal servant, disturbed him before he had rung himself. Nevertheless, as the half hour of ten struck, it occurred to Sybella that he was unusually late and she wondered how much Barbara Fallon's departure had to do with it.

How long had their argument carried on into the night after she had returned to her room? And what had Beatie heard that she would not reveal? She glanced idly along the corridor toward the door of the study. Had she been blind? she asked herself. Had everyone guessed at the relationship between Julian and Barbara Fallon? Had Ronnie known when he begged her not to marry his brother?

With a sudden feeling of surprise it dawned on her that light was entering the passage from the study door. It was so unlike Julian to leave his study door open that she moved forward and as she reached it she felt the unexpected rush of cold air from an open window. Frowning, she walked into the room. Directly in front of her the bottom sash of the wide, floor-to-ceiling window had been opened to its fullest extent, the heavy velvet curtaining blowing lazily into the room to reveal the garden behind. Shivering, she hurried forward and closed it.

It was only when she turned back to the door that her eyes rested upon Julian's desk on the right of the room and she glimpsed him sitting in his chair.

"Julian—!" His name died in her throat and she stood transfixed with horror, her eyes riveted upon the crimson stain on his shirtfront from where the glinting shaft of his silver letter opener protruded.

"Oh, my God!" she whispered. "Oh, my God!"

Chapter Four

The room was very cold. Crisp, brown leaves had blown in from the garden and were now lying scattered across the usually immaculate carpet. Alongside the writing desk the contents of an overturned decanter had formed a stain that almost matched the one upon Julian's shirt. Like someone in a trance Sybella continued to stare at Julian's body, unable to shift her eyes from the thin, silver handle of the letter opener, oblivious of the muffled sounds that escaped from her parched throat and incapable of summoning sufficient strength to run from the room.

From far off she heard her name being called. At first it was simply a distant echo that kept repeating itself in her head. Then, all at once, it exploded upon her consciousness and she felt fingers clutching at her arm.

"Sybella!"

She swung around and met Beatie's drawn, white face. "Oh, Beatie! Beatie!" She clung tightly to the old woman but Beatie said nothing as she quickly took in the scene before her, her lips compressed into a thin, straight line that controlled all signs of emotion. Only the piercing blue eyes seemed more than usually bright as they fastened upon the still form slumped in front of the writing desk.

"He's dead, Beatie," she whispered. "Julian is dead."

"Yes, child." She placed both hands upon Sybella's trembling shoulders and gently turned her away from Julian's body. "Don't look there any more. Dry your eyes now. Beatie is here to take care of everything."

Sybella nodded. She took a deep breath and struggled to regain her composure. She even attempted a small smile that was almost as quickly abandoned.

"I shall be all right." She wiped her eyes with the tips of her fingers and whispered shakily, "We must send for Dr. Carver."

"Yes. But first tell me what happened."

"I do not know, Beatie. I saw daylight streaming from the study into the passage and I thought perhaps Julian was working here. I came in and—" She broke off to stare at Beatie in shocked silence. The colour came flooding back into her pale face and her eyes flashed indignantly.

"Satan's oven!" she gasped. "You don't think *I* killed Julian!"

Beatie ruminated. "The possibility occurred to me," she finally admitted.

"*Thank you*!" Sybella scowled and began to pace the floor. For the first time since the shock of her discovery she was finding that her numbed brain was once again functioning of its own accord. She paused and when she spoke again her voice was quite controlled. "Beatie, Mrs. Fallon killed Julian," she said quietly.

"Sybella, you cannot say that with any surety!"

"Perhaps not—but nevertheless I *am* sure. They quarreled last night. I overhead them." She chose her words stiffly. "There was a relationship between them, Beatie. One we could never have suspected."

Beatice shaped her lips into a soundless "Oh." Then she said, "Barbara Fallon fell in love with your cousin, Sybella, the very first day she set foot in Rivers House."

"*You knew*!"

"Of course. Praise the Lord I still retain a few of my dwindling faculties."

Sybella shook her head in slow bewilderment. "I had no mind you knew of this," she whispered.

"Of course you didn't." Beatie's voice was gentle. "How could you? A young girl with all her dreams still in front of her. Only an old busybody like myself can quickly recognize such symptoms, even though it has always been at secondhand." She sucked in her cheeks with an expression of finality and bustled across to the window. "Now, let him rest, child," she said as she drew together the heavy velvet curtaining. "And be thankful that he is dead!"

"*Beatie!*"

"It is true. Have you not yet realized that your troubles no longer exist? Why, my child, you not only do not have to marry Julian Rivers but his property will surely be shared between yourself and Cousin Ronnie."

"Beatie, how *can* you! It is wicked to be talking like this with Julian dead."

"It is only because Julian is dead that we *can* talk like this! Now, we shall lock the door and give Jason instructions to summon Dr. Carver post-haste. It is for him to tell us what we must do next."

Sybella hesitated. "Before we summon Dr. Carver, Beatie, I believe I should hasten to the village by myself and inform Cousin Ronnie."

Beatie fumbled with the key for an excessively long time. "I feel certain Ronald will be most concerned," she murmured at last.

It was almost midday by the time Sybella arrived at the village and the marketplace was thronged with people despite the fine drizzle of rain that had plagued her all the way from Rivers House having now turned to a steady downpour. Chilled and damp in the open gig she had so thoughtlessly taken, Sybella dispiritedly steered her horse through the snare of traffic until she reached the shallow courtyard adjoining the Horse's Head.

The Horses's Head was the oldest establishment in the village and certainly the most picturesque. A wooden structure, it was set back from the marketplace and elevated above the storage cellars on ground level by a winding stairway leading to a gallery encompassing the entire building. It was common knowledge that all the rooms leading off the rear side of the gallery were permanently reserved for any gentleman requiring a discreet rendezvous, and as the fee charged was sufficiently exorbitant to discourage abuse by any uncouth element, the inn was able to boast an enviable reputation that was further enhanced by the rumour that it was regularly under royal patronage.

The innkeeper was a big, bluff countryman named Timothy Holt whom Sybella had known sufficiently well to acknowledge for as long as she could remember but she had never yet set foot in the inn and had certainly never contemplated doing so without a chaperon. As she hurried up the narrow stairway, the rain falling harder with every step she took, she heard the loud male laughter coming from the taproom and told herself that only the awful circumstances of the morning could have induced her to continue on with her visit now.

By the time Sybella had reached the shelter of the gallery, the spry little bunch of artificial white daisies on her delphinium blue bonnet was sagging dejectedly, her hair was clinging in lank strands to her cheeks and forehead, and a resourceful trickle of water had penetrated her cloak and was coursing uncomfortably down the back of her neck. A moment of indecision preceded her entrance through the door of the inn but it was quelled almost as it began by the icy gust that tugged at her skirts and started her teeth chattering.

In the centre of the small, cosy lounge Timothy Holt, a mug of ale in one fist, was gesticulating vehemently with the other at three local squires seated at a table and simultaneously contributing three contradictory opinions to an apparently incendiary topic. At the sight of Sybella silence descended upon the four men like a thick, woollen blanket.

Miserably aware of her unflattering appearance, Sybella deterred any possible exchange of ribaldry with an expression that might possibly have daunted an army. Never in her life before had she felt so self-conscious, both of herself and of her surroundings, but she mustered one last remaining shred of queenly dignity with which to address Timothy Holt.

"Good morning, Mr. Holt, I have come to see my cousin."

Timothy's eyes became saucers that were very nearly as round as his face.

"My cousin, Mr. Ronald Rivers. Would you kindly advise him that I am here?"

"Mr. Rivers—of course!" For a moment Timothy Holt's overawed expression failed to match the apparent comprehension in his voice. Then with an almighty effort he rallied.

"Good morning, Miss Howard! A very nasty morning indeed, eh? My word, you *are* wet!"

Sybella followed his eyes to the small puddle of water that had formed beside her on the carpet where she was standing and she blushed furiously.

"Mr. Holt," she snapped, "it is quite unnecessary for you to tell me what I already know! I would be far more grateful if you could find my cousin and tell him I am here."

"Beg pardon, Miss Howard." The poor man looked miserable, "—Er I'm afraid I've a bit of an upset for you."

"Mr. Holt, I truly do not understand you. What is it you are trying to say?"

"Mr. Ronald vacated his room here this morning."

"You mean he has left?"

"Yes, miss. He's gone to London. Drove himself, he did, in a regular beauty of a rig he won at the tables two nights ago. I wagered him he'd lose it again before the week was out—if you'll excuse me for saying so, miss—and he told me he'd send me word if he did or not. A real sport, Mr. Ronald, Miss Howard."

"Yes." Sybella formed the word soundlessly but there was no meaning in it. Only at this moment had she suddenly realized how much she had been relying upon Ronnie for support. She was so disappointed she quite failed to recollect the true reason for her journey to the Horse's Head nor realize that Ronnie's sudden and timely departure should merely have increased her initial fear that he might somehow be involved in Julian's death. But she was too

99

close to tears for any such thought to enter her head.

"Is there anything I can do?" Timothy Holt watched her with worried eyes.

"No, thank you, Mr. Holt." She forced a smile. "I expect I shall hear from my cousin within a day or so." She suddenly shivered and cast her eyes longingly towards the roaring log fire on the far side of the lounge. All pretence of grandeur deserted her. "Mr. Holt," she begged meekly, "would you please allow me to dry myself alongside your beautiful fire?"

"Indeed you may, Miss Howard, and I shall make you a stiff hot toddy to warm the inside as well as the outside. No, I shan't take any argument, so you just sit yourself down in that chair and make yourself comfy."

Sybella removed her wet cloak and bonnet and gloves and sank wearily down into the deep, comfortable chair in front of the fire. When Timothy returned a few minutes later with the promised hot toddy, she accepted it gratefully and as the healthy measure of Scotch whisky warmed her blood she started to feel better. Chiding herself for already having delayed so long in fetching. Dr. Carver, she quickly drained the last of her drink and got to her feet. To her horror, the moment she stood upright the room lurched to one side and her head began to swim alarmingly. She threw out her arms to steady herself and would certainly have fallen back into the chair she had just vacated had not two strong hands reached from behind to almost

100

completely encircle her waist.

It was not so much surprise but the unseemly pressure of the hands that shocked Sybella into instant sobriety. Then she heard his lazy, impudent voice ringing in her ears and the hot colour drenched her entire body as she realized Adam Brady was standing behind her.

"Isn't it a little early in the day to start tippling?" he remarked chattily.

Sybella spun around so quickly she almost lost her balance a second time but once again the strong fingers were around her waist to steady her.

"Perhaps you had better sit down again," he suggested helpfully.

"I overbalanced," she informed him testily. At the same time she tried desperately to deal surreptitiously with her hair which had dried into a mass of tangled curls. Forcing herself to look up into his handsome face, she saw his dark eyes crinkling with amusement at her predicament, and grinding her white teeth miserably, she picked up her bonnet and jammed it unceremoniously on top of the offending curls.

"I shouldn't bother," he assured her gravely. "I think you look perfectly delightful just the way you are."

"You are teasing me," she stammered.

He shook his head and Sybella raised her eyes once more to his. He stood before her, making no attempt to remove his hands from about her waist, tall and slender in the perfectly tailored breeches and top boots he seemed to

101

favour in preference to the pantaloons and Hessians generally worn by London gentlemen. She allowed her eyes to close as the pressure of his hands increased and her heart pounded as she felt herself being drawn gradually closer to his body. Then, with a movement so abrupt that her eyes snapped open with surprise, he planted her firmly back on her own two feet and released her from his hold.

"Now, what are you doing here?" he asked conversationally.

"I—I—came to see my cousin, Ronald Rivers." Sybella bit off the words edgily.

"He isn't here any more."

"So I have been informed."

"I know your cousin well."

"How nice for him." She suddenly recalled just how long Adam Brady had been in the village and she frowned angrily as she realized how a few moments ago she had longed for his kisses, yet he actually thought so little of her that he had never even bothered to deliver his card.

"I suppose you have been the influence encouraging Ronnie to gamble," she added acidly.

"You don't approve of gambling?"

"Not when one has to borrow to pay one's debts."

"But Ronnie had plenty of money—at least he did this week." He grinned. "That is why I suggested he go to London—whilst he still had it. I have loaned him the use of my rooms in Brook Street."

"Ronnie is staying at your apartment? Oh, please—give me the address so that I may write to him immediately."

"Of course." His eyes narrowed and he took her hand and held it firmly between his own. "You are in trouble, aren't you." She did not answer and he sought her eyes gently. "You might ask me for help, you know."

Sybella shook her head. "I could not presume to burden you with my troubles." She tried to wriggle her fingers from his grasp but he refused to free her.

"Ask me," he whispered.

"No—I—Oh, Adam—!" The strain of the day suddenly proved too much for her. She felt the tears brimming and she tried desperately to stem them but it was already too late. Adam drew her closer, his arms went about her shoulders, and with a strangled sob Sybella buried her face against his chest.

He waited until her sobbing had subsided, then he gently tilted her face and dried her eyes with his pocket handkerchief. "Do you feel better now?" he asked her. She nodded and he went on softly. "Do you want to tell me what is troubling you?"

"Yes." She swallowed hard. "Oh, yes, I do!"

"Tell me, then."

Sybella hesitated just a moment longer than in a voice only just a little above a whisper the whole story tumbled out. "I wanted to find Ronnie first—before I called Dr. Carver—but

103

now I must do it by myself. Adam—tell me what to do!''

"I am going to take you back home to Rivers House at once.'' He picked up her cloak and threw it around her shoulders and hurried her out of the inn.

They took Adam's curricle, having decided to leave the gig at the inn's stables, and they were well on the road to Rivers House before Adam made any further mention of the tragedy. "Did you see any sign of the assailant, Sybella?'' he asked her quietly.

She shook her head. "I saw nothing—but I am readily certain that Julian was slain by Barbara Fallon, the housekeeper.''

It seemed to Sybella that an air of unreality had hung over the entire morning but this feeling was quickly dissipated upon her return to Rivers House for even the house itself exuded an atmosphere of foreboding. It was all she could do to force herself to enter the study with Adam and she found it impossible to direct her eyes to the desk. But it was wasted effort because the scene was so engraved upon her memory she could see it all again anyway.

Sybella turned her back and left Adam standing beside the body where he remained for some time finally crossing to her. "Who knows about this?'' he asked her quietly.

"Only Beatie—nobody else.''

"You are certain?''

"Quite certain." He nodded with apparent satisfaction and she studied his face with puzzled eyes. "I don't understand," she faltered.

"Of course you don't." He smiled at her gently. "And I am afraid I cannot enlighten you—not yet." He paused and when he spoke again his voice carried a note of deadly seriousness. "Sybella can you trust me? Can you put your faith in my hands?"

"Yes," she whispered, "but—"

"And ask me no questions until I am in a position to volunteer the answers?"

"Yes, but—"

"Will you promise me?"

"Yes, I promise you, but—"

"But what?" He smiled crookedly.

"Shouldn't we go at once to Dr. Carver?" He shook his head and she looked at him helplessly. "Well," she frowned worriedly, "what are you going to do? Can I ask that question?"

"Not really—but I will tell you that I am going to move Julian's body away from Rivers House."

"Oh, no!" She stared at him aghast. "Adam, you couldn't!"

"You promised me that you could trust me," he reminded her.

"Yes, I know, but if you do this," her voice was small and filled with misery, "whoever killed Julian may never be brought to trial."

"If you are referring to Mrs. Fallon, I prom-

ise you that you need have no fear. If she killed
your cousin, she will pay for it. But trust me. Is
it so impossible?''

"I do trust you, Adam—but if you are seen—"

"Don't worry!"

"How can I not worry? If you had any sense,
you would be worrying with me!"

He grinned at her boyishly and her heart
somersaulted and she experienced a wave of
guilt that she should feel so happy just to have
Adam Brady smile at her like that when Julian
was huddled in death only a few feet away from
them.

"Now," he said, "will you go and see if the
way is clear for me to take out the body?
Oh—and I shall need his coat and hat."

Sybella nodded her head. She was at the door
when he stopped her.

"Sybella—you would not have married Julian,
would you?"

She stood quite still but she did not turn
around to face him. "No," she answered carefully, "I would not have married Julian."

"I am glad," he said, and without another
word he let her go. Ten minutes later he was on
his way to his undisclosed destination with the
body of Julian Rivers.

Acting upon Adam's instructions, Sybella
informed the servants that Julian had gone to
London on urgent business. If they considered it
titillating that Barbara Fallon should have done
the same thing and chosen the same evening to
do it, no word or action betrayed their interest

and all scandalmongering was decorously confined to the kitchen.

On the other hand, Sybella found it quite impossible to follow Adam's instructions concerning herself. She felt she could not carry on with the now farcical wedding plans and she postponed as many of them as she was decently able to do without arousing comment. However, with time now lying idle on her hands, she was forced to spend each interminable hour anxiously waiting for word to come from Adam or reliving the horror of discovering Julian's body. On top of this she discovered she had Beatie to contend with in one of her most militant moods.

Three mornings after the murder she was sitting in her bedroom, a pink peignoir thrown over her night attire, idly buffing her nails, when Beatie entered.

"Good morning, Beatie." Sybella met Beatie's forbidding expression and wearily returned to her polishing.

"You haven't eaten your breakfast!"

"I've had all I wish," Sybella murmured quietly.

"It isn't sufficient."

"I'm not hungry."

"That isn't surprising." Beatie was haphazardly gathering clothes and flinging them helter-skelter into the soiled linen basket. "What with the angel of death hovering over our heads for days on end, it would be a blessed miracle if either of us had an appetite!"

Sybella flung down her nail buff with an

exclamation of impatience. "Truly, Beatie, I do declare that each day finds you more tiresome than the last!"

Beatie bristled. "Tiresome, indeed! I expect I am also to blame for the pretty pickle we are in at this moment!"

"Mr. Brady is a gentleman and I have the utmost faith in him. I am quite sure that whatever he has done has been with our best interests at heart."

"And what, pray tell me," Beatie put in waspishly, "has your fine gentleman done?"

"Never fear, we shall be informed in due course."

"It is now four days."

"There is a reason."

"What reason? Moreover, what lawful reason could any man have for hiding a body for even one day? The man is obviously a rogue! A good-looking rogue, I grant you, but still a rogue!" An extra thought occurred to her and her eyes widened in sudden horror. "Great heavens, child! The next step will be blackmail—mark my words!"

"*Really, Beatie*! I swear your imagination is becoming sufficiently rich for you to try your pen at one of those penny papers."

"You can scoff but tell me what you know about your fine Mr. Brady. Who is he and what does he do? Do you know? And even if he has told you, I warrant it is a pack of lies! What is more, you should at least confide in your cousin Ronald."

"I gave Mr. Brady my word I would confide in no one."

"Ronald is Julian's brother, his closest relative, and he should know!"

"Beatie, I promised."

"Then you had no right to do so. Go to the Horse's Head and tell him you have changed your mind!"

"Beatie, how can I possibly do that?"

"Easy! I shall go with you and show you!"

Sybella sighed and shook her head. "No, I shall go to the village by myself."

"Very well, but Jason can drive you. I'll go and find him." She paused. "It is a cold morning. What are you wearing?"

Sybella smiled and it was the first genuine smile she had been able to manage for three full days. "Strangely enough, Beatie darling, all the clean clothing you have now jammed so securely into your soiled linen basket."

Despite her assertion that she was agreeing to go and see Adam merely to salve Beatie's ill-humour, Sybella secretly welcomed the suggestion as an opportunity to dispel her own gently nagging doubts. Besides which it gave her something to do with her day other than to spend it waiting and worrying.

As the carriage drew nearer the marketplace, she experienced a sudden panic that something might have happened to Adam and that when she went to the inn she would not find him. Without waiting to give Jason instructions where he should wait for her, she flung out of the carriage and pushing her way through the jostling market crowd she hurried up the narrow wooden stairway of the Horse's Head. With courage born from her previous visit, she swept confidently into the small, deserted lounge and after only a moment's hesitation rang loudly for attention. Within seconds Timothy Holt himself appeared.

"Bless my bones, if it isn't Miss Howard! A mite dryer than last visit, eh, miss? Well now, did you hear from Mr. Ronald?"

"Thank you, Mr. Holt." Sybella smiled affably. "I must confess I did not apologize to you for being such a nuisance. Please accept my excuses now, will you?"

"Ah, you were no trouble at all." He blushed furiously for such a red-faced man and changed the subject. "What can I do for you?"

"I would like to see Mr. Brady. Is he still here at the inn?"

"Yes, he is, Miss Howard—but only until this evening."

"Oh." She rushed on, her mind whirling, aware that he was waiting curiously. "Er—do you mind telling him I am here?"

"Can't do that, miss. I'm afraid he's gone out." He pulled at his ear thoughtfully. "I believe he muttered something about he might send someone to collect his luggage and pay his bill if he didn't come back."

"But—but I might miss him then?"

"Sorry, Miss Howard. P'raps, if it's very important, you could wait here on the chance of

110

him coming in or leave a message with me."

"Isn't there any other way? Haven't you any idea where I could find him? It is very important."

"Well, I suppose he could be at the Brown Hen at this time of the day. You might try there although it isn't the best place in the town for a lady to be seen in, if you know what I mean, Miss Howard."

Sybella nodded her head impatiently. "This Brown Hen—where is it?"

"It's a coffeehouse in Morton Street—a couple of turnings left off the marketplace." He indicated the general direction with his thumb. "But I'm not at all sure it wouldn't be a better idea to wait right here."

Sybella flashed him a brilliant smile. "Thank you, Mr. Holt. If I do not find Mr. Brady, I shall certainly accept your kind offer." Then with a quick turn she hurried from the room.

Anxious now and determined that she must find Adam Brady before he went away, Sybella hastened through the crowds. Morton Street, which she finally located with only a small degree of difficulty, turned out to be little more than a rather grubby alleyway, a hundred yards or so away from the main marketplace, and the coffeehouse, though fragrantly advertised well in advance, was even less prepossessing. A single-story wooden structure, it was held up by a deserted feed store on one side and a building on the other that appeared to have been gutted by fire some years before and never rebuilt. The whole area seemed unpleasantly cut off and noiseless and the gentle rumble of traffic from the marketplace merely accentuated the silence.

With thudding heart Sybella hesitated, miserably uncertain of what she should do. She moved slowly forward and rubbed cautiously at the misted glass of the large, bow windows with the tips of her gloved fingers. Peering through, she could see a dark brown interior of cubicles, wooden tables and benches, set out in four evenly spaced rows. But because they were cubicles, she could see only a few of the customers' faces. The atmosphere appeared to be orderly but it was obvious with one glance that it was not a place for an unescorted lady. She hesitated a moment longer and then with a gesture of impatience with her own indecision she squared her shoulders and walked quickly to the door and opened it.

The foul stench of hot air and tobacco smoke struck her full in the face with all the force of a second door, and for an instant she stood dazed, struggling to regain her so recently acquired bravado.

A waiter passed her with a tray of empty cups. He glanced at her significantly but said nothing. When he returned a few minutes later, she was still standing in the same spot.

He paused. "You can't stand here."

"I'm sorry—I'm looking for someone."

He shrugged his shoulders. "Who isn't? But you still can't stand here." He indicated an empty cubicle with his tray. "Sit down. I'll bring you a coffee."

"No, please—I am looking for a particular gentleman. Perhaps you can help me? His name is Adam Brady—a very tall man. Big. Very dark hair. He might be here."

"He might. I don't know him. Take a walk if you want to look for him. But don't cause any trouble!"

Hot with embarrassment and sick and tired of her own impetuosity that seemed to be forever involving her in these impossible situations, Sybella moved awkwardly down the narrow thoroughfare between the two left-hand rows of cubicles. The cubicles were by no means all occupied and it took her less than a minute to satisfy herself that Adam Brady was not seated in any of them.

With a sense of urgency in her movements she started along the other section, oblivious now of everything else except her purpose. She had only taken a few steps when her heart suddenly soared and a smile broke spontaneously upon her lips. His well-defined, black brows drawn close together in deep concentration, he was paying close attention to what his companion was saying. They were seated at the end of the passageway in the second to last cubicle by the front door, and Sybella hastened her steps. As she did so, she suddenly glimpsed the features of the other man and recognized him instantly. She hesitated, endeavouring to recollect the man's name before reaching the cubicle, but it eluded her although she felt vaguely certain that he had something to do with her holiday in France. She had met so many of her aunt's and uncle's friends she was about to dismiss the problem and continue forward when her heart suddenly froze and she stood rooted to the spot as remembrance flashed across her mind like a warning bell. *The intruder from the Tête de Boeuf*!

She told herself that she was mad, that it was nothing but a trick of light, a similarity, her overwrought imagination playing her false. But even as she made these excuses to herself, she was running in blind panic back towards the rear of the room, through a doorway, oblivious of the stunned astonishment of kitchen staff, oblivious of everything except the knowledge that she must escape unseen from Adam Brady.

She felt the cold air strike her cheeks but she kept running until she could run no longer and she stopped, exhausted, to regain her breath. It was only then that she realized she had turned left at the rear of the coffeehouse and was now at the end of a blind alley. With tears of dismay welling in her eyes, she turned wearily back the way she had just come.

She had passed the Brown Hen and was just about to turn right into what she believed would eventually lead into Morton Street when it happened. Later Sybella realized that everything had happened simultaneously although at the time all she was conscious of was the cruel, smothering hand that gripped hard across her nose and mouth.

"*Watch out, miss!*" The man who uttered the warning cry seemed to appear from nowhere but within seconds the deserted alley had sprung to life as windows rattled open and the back doors of buildings swung inwards. Sybella never saw her assailant. Even as she heard his whispered curse and felt his warm breath upon her cheek, she was falling forward onto the cobbles where he had pushed her.

"Are you hurt?" The stranger, a bookish-looking young man in his late twenties, had reached her and was helping her to her feet. She could feel her knees stinging where the cobbles had grazed them but she shook her head and forced a weak smile, anxious now to get away before more interest was aroused and other people gathered. She stooped and picked up her bonnet and hurriedly brushed down her dishevelled attire while the young man watched her admiringly.

"Who was he? Where did he go?" Her rescuer was hot with fervour. "Please let me escort you home."

"Thank you, but I have a carriage waiting." She smiled again and this time genuine warmth was reflected on her face. "I am so very grateful to you, sir. It was very brave of you to come to my aid as you did."

"I wish I could have caught him! There's

been a lot of robbing from unattended ladies these past months. You were lucky. He didn't get a chance to grab your purse, did he?''

"No, I was lucky. Now I must go.'' She bowed and without another word turned and hurried away. Yes, she was lucky. She knew that now. But her assailant had not been in any way interested in stealing her purse—she knew that also.

All the way home Sybella made her plans. She had made up her mind what she must do—she had to find Ronnie and she would leave for London on the first coach, which was to-morrow morning. Badly shaken though she had been by Julian's murder, she had, nevertheless, been able to come to terms with the tragedy, partially because of the mystery surrounding it having absorbed all her thoughts and also because Adam Brady had shouldered all responsibility. But now the tide had turned alarmingly and for some inexplicable reason she had become the target of destruction. She was frightened and bewildered by it all but this was nothing in comparison with her discovery that Adam Brady was part of it.

As the carriage raced and swayed along the uneven dirt road to Rivers House, Sybella's cheeks were wet with tears. Adam Brady had come to mean more to her than any man she had ever known and it filled her with shame that she could have been so easily deceived. For, from that first evening in Paris, when he had been seen leaving—*and not entering*—her bed-room, their relationship had been a lie which had finally culminated in Julian's death and the frightening assault on herself. *But why? To what purpose?* They were the questions that kept on pounding in her head.

Beatie was waiting for her when she arrived. She took one quick glance at Sybella's face and her eyes narrowed.

"What happened?" she asked sharply.

"Nothing." She feigned surprise.

"Did you *see* him?"

"Oh, yes, of course." She gave Beatie a gentle peck on the cheek and hurried past her on the staircase.

"Well? Aren't you going to tell me what he said?"

"Beatie, I'm going to find Ronnie. I'm going to take the early morning stage to London."

"Thank heaven for that!" She allowed her-self a tiny smile of satisfaction before reflecting further. "Did Mr. Brady suggest this to you?"

"No, it was my own idea."

Beatie sniffed. "It was mine, but no matter. The important thing is what explanation did he give you? What is he doing?"

"Beatie, I don't *know*!" The reply sounded as if it had been wrenched from her and she ran the few remaining steps to her bedroom. There she turned, her emotions once again controlled but her unhappiness clearly mirrored on her face. "I'm sorry, Beatie. I promise to explain

117

everything to you before long. Just be a dear, now, and fetch me my small trunk. I must start packing as soon as possible."

With immeasurable difficulty Beatie curbed her tongue. Then her eyebrows lifted in mild alarm as her thoughts sped on ahead. "You are not planning on travelling to London alone, are you?"

"I am and you know very well I have no other choice. Someone has to stay here and there is only you to do so."

Slightly mollified, Beatie's sense of fitness still needed to be assuaged.

"Where will you stay?" she asked.

"Grillons." Sybella was already hurling clothes from the wardrobe onto the bed.

"Grillons! It is not the thing to go there unattended."

"Truly, Beatie, I am quite past giving a fig what is the thing to do! If Grillons refuse to accept me, then I shall find someone else who will!"

Sybella heard a carriage coming up the drive an hour or so later but she paid no particular heed to it and when a knock sounded on her bedroom door not long afterwards she did not even bother to raise her eyes from her packing.

"Come in, Beatie," she murmured. "I have almost finished."

There was a short silence whilst Sybella spread tissue paper over the top of her packing before he spoke.

"It isn't Beatie."

The colour slowly draining from her cheeks, she looked up to face Adam Brady's quizzical expression.

"You are planning a journey?" he asked smiling.

"What are you doing here?" She groped painfully for the words.

His eyes flickered uncertainly as he regarded her but his manner remained quietly casual.

"Aren't you expecting me?"

Sybella rose to her feet from the kneeling position she had adopted beside her trunk. Taking a deep breath to steady herself, she faced him defiantly.

"Yes, I was expecting you, Mr. Brady, but I am ashamed to say I was frightened to admit it—even to myself. Wasn't that foolish of me? But then you know how foolish I am, don't you? I am also very inexperienced—but of course you know that also."

Adam Brady hunched his big shoulders helplessly. "I am slowly beginning to think that I know nothing any more."

"You are too modest, Mr. Brady—but let me tell you this. I have no idea whatsoever what it is you want from me nor what this awful nightmare is all about, but I want you to know that I am not afraid any more and if that is further proof of my foolishness I am quite sure you will derive even greater amusement from it. Now please leave my room. I have much to do."

119

For a moment Adam looked at her in complete silence, a hint of admiration lurking in his dark eyes, before he shook his head in helpless bewilderment.

"What in the devil's name are you talking about?" he demanded.

"There is no need to pretend any longer, Mr. Brady. Now I do not know how you succeeded in persuading Beatie to allow you to come to my bedroom but I do wish you would now please go."

"I am not going anywhere until I find out what all this nonsense is about! Who the devil has been filling your head with rubbish?"

"*Please*, Mr. Brady!"

"Now you listen to me, Sybella Howard!" He took a step towards her.

"Don't you dare come any closer to me!"

"Sybella—have you gone completely mad?"

"On the contrary, I have gone completely sane!"

"What happened this afternoon? Who did you see? I know you were in the village searching for me, Timothy Holt told me so."

"Then you should have no difficulty in realizing what I discovered!"

"My dear girl, I am beginning to have difficulty in realizing my own sanity!"

"I saw *you*—in that place—and I saw your companion—and I *recognized* him—as I am sure you must know only too well. Perhaps it was even you—who tr—tried to—to—" Her eyes

120

smarted unbearably and her voice, despite her frantic attempts to control it, started to waver dangerously. Then there was nothing she could do. The sobs, the fears and anxiety that had been denied an outlet for so long finally became too much for her to withhold any longer.

"Sybella! What is it?" Gripping her shaking shoulders, he struggled to comfort her but she fought him desperately, her body writhing in his arms.

"Please!" she begged tearfully. "Please— don't—hurt—me!"

"*Hurt you! You little fool!*" Then his mouth was hard upon hers, his arms crushing her tightly against the lean length of his body. "I love you," he whispered. "God knows I would never harm you." He held her from him and looked close into her tear-filled eyes. "You do believe that, don't you?"

"Oh, I want to believe it—so terribly."

"What happened, my darling? Forget the man you saw me with—what else happened? It is important that I should know."

"Someone—a man—I don't know—" she looked at Adam appealingly, "after I saw you in the coffeehouse, someone tried to kill me! I know he tried—he would have I am sure if he hadn't been disturbed. Adam—what is it all about?" Her voice rose shrilly. "I *am* frightened. And you *know*—you *must* know. All these things that have been happening—the intruder who was searching my luggage—Julian's mur-

121

der—it is all connected, isn't it? But *me*—why do they want to kill *me*? Adam, tell me please—what can I do to stop it?" Her voice was pleading. "You must tell me!"

"Yes." He nodded his head slowly. "I believe it is time you were told a great deal."

Chapter Five

"Hush, now. No more tears." Adam gently dried her eyes with his pocket handkerchief.

For some minutes Sybella seemed to be perfectly contented just to lie in his arms, the wonder of being there temporarily obscuring the circumstances by which it had happened, until gradually her body started to grow tense once more as recollection began to return.

"Adam," she whispered, "somebody tried to kill me! You do believe that don't you?"

"Yes—I do."

There was something present in his voice or in the hesitancy of his reply that instantly alerted her and put her on her guard, but even though she was waiting expectantly for his next words, she was totally unprepared for them when they came.

"I am afraid, my dear, I am even to blame for it."

Sybella stared at him dumbly, almost as if the words had been uttered in a foreign tongue. Then, as the full measure of meaning dawned upon her, all her old fears were released once more to feast upon her bewildered mind.

Adam patted her hand carelessly, completely unaware of the turmoil his words had summoned.

"Remember, I said there was much you should be told."

With a little cry of alarm she wrenched herself free and hurried towards the door.

"Please leave my bedchamber," she directed him steadfastly. "Go now before I summon help."

Adam grinned cheerfully. "Who did you have in mind to call? Jason or Beatie? I must confess to being a trifle chary of Miss Beatie." He held out his arms to her in conciliatory fashion. "Come now, my darling, I excuse you for feeling some irritation of the nerves in learning of my involvement in this matter, but, after all, I am not entirely to blame for your upsetting experience, am I? I cannot believe you were unaware that a certain amount of risk was inevitable when you foolishly chose to take part in the scheme."

Sybella shaded her eyes with trembling fingers. "Either I am dreaming all this," she gasped, "or you have entirely taken leave of your senses!"

124

"Come, Sybella," a slight testiness crept into his voice, "I haven't the slightest intention of betraying you to the authorities and well you know it. Therefore I see no point in your apparent insistence upon fencing with me."

"Indeed you *are* mad!"

"*Sybella!*"

"How *dare* you shout at me!" She made a lunge for the handle of the door. "I am leaving this instant."

"Sybella—*please*!" The urgency in his voice forced her to turn back instinctively and he took advantage of the moment to cross to her and take her hand. "Assure me," he begged her, "in all sincerity that you are completely ignorant of all that my words have implied."

"Of course I assure you!" she snapped.

"The *deuce*!" He stared down at her for a moment in utter astonishment, his dark eyes bright with unexpected pleasure, then his brow darkened and he started to pace the floor with great agitation.

"Now what is the matter?" Sybella demanded irritably.

"What you have just told me might just possibly change a certain aspect rather considerably," he murmured thoughtfully.

"It changes nothing! It merely adds further to my confusion. I beg you to kindly grant me the charity of your long promised explanation."

"Sit down."

"I prefer to stand, thank you."

125

"Sybella—do you no longer trust me?"

"I—I truly it is most difficult for me to answer—how can I—"

"If you do not give your trust to me, you will indeed be fortunate if you find another whom you can."

"What do you mean by that?" Sybella's voice faltered.

"Sit down and I shall try to explain."

She obeyed him meekly and just as meekly allowed him to hold her hand as he sat down beside her and started his discourse.

"Sybella, did it ever occur to you to consider in what direction your aunt's and uncle's sympathies were directed during the war between England and France?"

"They never lived in France," she retorted quickly. "Their home was in Switzerland for the greater part of that period."

"So I believe. They also have many influential friends which accounts for a great deal. However, it does not quite answer my question, except that in my experience I have found that an expatriate, in times of national strife, can be more fervently patriotic than any of his brothers at home."

"Politics have never interested either my aunt or my uncle; they have assured me of this on a number of occasions. Besides," Sybella thought fondly of the soft plump features of her Aunt Sophie and the kindly, fine-looking face of her Uncle Philippe, and she snapped her eyes

126

decisively, "your inferences are quite out of hand."

"Perhaps they are. However, the Servais household has been under constant surveillance for some considerable time and it is a positive fact that somebody there has been passing and receiving information from a French agent in England."

"Satan's oven! You talk as if we were still at war!"

"We are still at war! Despite the testimony of an infamous piece of paper called the Treaty of Amiens, Napoleon has no more intention of living by that treaty than he has of living in peace with the rest of Europe."

"This is too much. You almost ruined my farewell ball with these same absurd notions. Who are you, Adam Brady, to say such things?"

"Sybella," he spoke very quietly, "I am an agent employed by our government and I tell you of this only because I love you and because it is imperative that you trust me."

Her eyes rounded and she experienced a sharp stab of excitement. "Are you a spy?" she breathed.

Adam smiled. "If it gives you pleasure to use the word—then I am a spy."

"Oh." She paused and looked at him, suddenly helpless. "But what has it all got to do with me?" she asked.

"A great deal. Eight days after your departure to Paris, we received information advising us that the French agent in England, who was providing the direct link with the Servais household, had finally been uncovered. His name was Lord Rivers, your cousin, Sybella.''

''Julian? Why, I don't believe it!''

''It is true nevertheless. You, yourself, unknowingly, provided us with the final positive proof we needed.''

''I did!'' Sybella regarded Adam with disbelief. ''How?''

''It was an extremely simple plan—and devilishly difficult to uncover.''

''I see.'' She lowered her eyes thoughtfully. When she spoke, her voice was strangely flat. ''It wasn't by chance that you were at my ball in Paris, was it, Adam.''

''Indeed, no. Your presence in the Servais household was a piece of good fortune we had never anticipated. We were quite certain that you would be used, either voluntarily or otherwise, to carry information back to Julian and it was essential that someone should be on hand to intercept it.''

''You had been searching my bedchamber that last evening in Paris, hadn't you? You were seen leaving by my window and you pretended to me that you had come from another part of the wing.''

''So, my chicanery has been uncovered!'' He grinned cheerfully. ''I trust you will not hold it against me.''

''Why should I do that?'' Sybella's voice was

dangerously pleasant but Adam noticed nothing amiss.

"You must have been in my chambers for the better portion of twenty minutes," she went on.

"Er—give or take a few seconds."

"I compliment you upon your stealth."

"Practice."

"And did you discover what you were looking for?"

"No."

"*Ha!*"

"What did you say?"

"I said *ha!*"

"And pray what does that signify?"

"It signifies, Mr. Brady. that you spent twenty fruitless minutes invading my privacy and endangering my reputation, following which you and your equally odious companion spent the next three days of my journey to Calais persecuting me, disordering my luggage, and cruelly assaulting my frail and elderly abigail!"

"My dear Miss Howard, I would like to remind you that I am not the enemy! You may recall in that feeble brain of yours that I told you I worked for the British Government. If you would care to pause for a moment's consideration, I am sure you might well realize that we are both on the same side!"

"How do I know you are speaking the truth? How do I know anything? If you are indeed what you say you are, why didn't you tell me then? I would have willingly aided you."

129

"I rather doubt that you would have trusted me more so at that time and to be perfectly frank, my dear, I would not have trusted you."

Sybella glowered and changed the subject. "You mentioned that I provided proof of Julian's guilt. I conclude from that remark that you discovered something."

"I did."

"May I ask what?"

"If you would cease being so prickly, I would tell you all in an easy fashion! It so happens that you were carrying a coded list of the names of twelve new French agents domiciled in this country plus valuable confirmation of information we had already received from other sources concerning Napoleon's invasion plans."

Sybella gasped. "I never carried any such message!"

"Yes, you did, in the hollowed handle of your pretty little shot-silk sunshade and when you arrived at Rivers House it was received by Julian as planned—with whom we do not know yet for certain. Julian in turn conveyed this message—now carrying several revisions made by myself on behalf of the War Office—to yet a further destination. Regretfully the tampered-with section of the message was detected and unhappily for Julian he became the natural suspect and he paid for this imagined duplicity with his life."

"No!" Sybella shook her head violently. "Barbara Fallon murdered Julian!"

"No, Sybella. Barbara Fallon had nothing

whatever to do with your cousin's death, I assure you of that. Julian's murderer was apprehended several hours before you even discovered his body." He regarded her shamefacedly. "Yes, I am afraid I was also forced to mislead you with regard to this matter, but I was under orders. Your cousin's death had to remain undiscovered for as long as possible so that we could repair the danger that had been done. When he is found in the next day or two, it will be reported that he died from injuries sustained in a fall from a horse. I'm sorry, my dear."

She shook her head miserably. "How horrible it all is," she whispered. "And I cannot understand why he did this. Julian was never sympathetic to France. Why should he be willing to betray his own country?"

"For money, Sybella."

"But Julian was an extremely rich man!"

"On the contrary. He was a very poor one and sadly in debt."

Sybella pressed one hand against her temple.

"Oh, this passes everything!" she exclaimed. "You have made me feel just like a cork bobbing up and down in the middle of the ocean!"

"Upon my honour I wish it were otherwise."

"*You* wish it!" She closed her eyes distractedly. "To think that if I had never met you, I would at this moment be—be—" She continued no further as colour suffused her cheeks.

"Preparing for your marriage to Julian?" Adam finished the sentence for her.

She tossed her curls, both angry and embarrassed that he should already know her sufficiently well as to be able to read her thoughts. An instant later a worried frown was again creasing her brow.

"You have not yet explained why anyone should wish to harm me. Surely I too am not suspected of—of double-dealings?"

Adam shook his head slowly. "I just don't know, Sybella. Frankly I cannot understand how your murder could be anything else but a pointless and quite unnecessary danger to our opponents. In fact, as far as anyone can know at present, you are still a very valuable asset to the Servais household."

"I find it in distinctly bad taste the manner in which you can calmly sit next to me and casually discuss my possible murder!"

"You asked me a question and I gathered you required an answer. However, if it puts your mind at rest, I do believe that whatever the danger was, it is over now?"

"Do you really believe that?"

"I do. Come now, let me see you smile."

"In all truth I have never felt less like smiling in my entire life."

"I can well believe that, my love, but the effort will help you to feel better." She squeezed a tremulous little smile and he nodded his head approvingly. "There! Don't you feel a little better already?"

"No. But I realize you speak this way to me out of kindness. You have been most frank with me, Adam. I am indeed grateful."

"May I take it then that you are no longer put out with me?" The old devilish, half-taunting grin was back on his face again.

"You are a man used to having his own way. In such a small matter I see no reason why I should prolong a discussion by bothering to disagree."

He chuckled happily. "You possess admirable spirit for a female, my love. It is a shame that you are going to be tamed."

"That *you* will never do, sir!"

"We shall see about that when this wretched affair is finalised." He rose to his feet, ignoring her attempts to find a suitable answer. "I must bid you adieu," he murmured lightly.

"Oh!" Her face fell. "You are returning to the village?"

"I must."

"But—"

"You shall be safe, I promise you. The moment I arrive there, I shall make arrangements for Harris," he smiled, "my odious assistant, to come here. He will look after you."

"Then you *do* believe there is still danger."

"No—but it is fine practice for Harris." He brushed her fingers with his lips. "I shall endeavour to return by midday tomorrow with positive news that will put your mind completely at rest."

The grandfather clock had just chimed eight when Robert Harris presented his credentials to Sybella in the drawing room where she was vainly endeavouring to engage her mind in her needlework. On closer inspection, Robert Harris turned out to be a short and stocky gentleman, pleasant of countenance, noticeably muscular, of an indeterminate age beyond forty years and with an astonishingly mild manner and shy demeanour. In fact, Sybella felt substantially foolish now that she recalled her previous sinister judgment of him, and her greeting was slightly more cordial than necessary to compensate for it. On the other hand, Beatie's welcome was, perhaps understandably, a shade cooler, but Sybella's earlier graphic account of the maelstrom into which they had both been so unwittingly flung had left Beatie so undone that an offer of protection from Lucifer himself would have received grateful consideration had it arrived first.

"May I offer you some light refreshment, Mr. Harris?" Sybella asked.

Robert Harris shook his head. "You are very kind but I merely wished to make my presence known to you and gather a little information concerning the household. Tell me, who is here beside you two ladies?"

Sybella carefully enumerated the servants. "There is Jason who looks after the horses and who is our coachman. His quarters are next to the stables. Then there is my late cousin's valet, John, who also helps with the household chores; Mrs. Haddock, the cook, and her husband. They have a young daughter who also does some of
134

the housework. The housekeeper, Mrs. Fallon, is no longer with us.''

''Nobody else? No gardeners for instance?''

''Two—but they come each day from the village.''

Robert nodded his head with apparent satisfaction. ''Now, I will request you two ladies to forget that I am here.''

''I wish that were possible,'' Sybella answered with a slight smile.

''I give you my word you will sleep undisturbed.''

Beatie's sharp blue eyes lingered upon her former adversary liverishly.

''Nevertheless, I shall myself bolt all doors and windows, Mr. Harris.''

''A wise decision, Miss Crewe. Let us all trust you will be bolting the danger out—and not locking it in. Goodnight.''

He bowed to Sybella and as his glance fell upon Beatie's murderous frown, his left eyelid seemed to tremble into what Beatie could have sworn later looked exactly like a wink.

''What do you think he is going to do now?'' demanded Beatie uncertainly, the moment the door had closed behind him.

Sybella sighed. ''He said he was going to guard us.''

''But can we trust him?''

''If he had wished to murder us, dear, it would have been simpler for him to accomplish it before being locked outside, wouldn't it?''

"Devious eyes spawn devious plans," Beatie intoned prophetically.

"Be that as it may, I have no desire to discuss the wretched business further. I have an edition of the *Lady's Magazine* and I propose to read it from cover to cover and then proceed to bed where I shall sleep."

But it was a long time before sleep came. For, despite her confident avowal to Beatie, the moment she had lowered the oil lamp beside her bed, her thoughts were spinning, recapturing every word of the fantastic story that Adam Brady had confided. She buried her face in the pillow, trying to blot out of her mind the final picture it held of her cousin Julian, but she could not. How was it possible, she asked herself, to have known Julian so well and to have known so little about him? Was it like that with everybody? With Ronnie? With Beatie? With Adam?

It was raining heavily when Sybella awoke the next morning, but despite her lack of sleep and the miserable appearance of the day she was unable to deny herself her mood of blithe spirits. After a light breakfast she shooed Beatie from the room and promptly shut herself in. She chose her prettiest gown of lime green velvet which she knew set off her raven hair to advantage and took an absurd length of time over her toilet. She was still paying one last regard to her appearance when she heard the long awaited approach of horses on the carriageway and on an impulse suddenly touched each cheek with a fleck of rouge. As she instantly rubbed it off again, there was little enough cause for concern at her behaviour and, happily, the friction of her outraged fingers added to the hot flush of guilt that Adam might notice the artifice, created the desired effect anyway.

She smiled up at him bewitchingly as she led him to the drawing room, but a slight furrow was already marking her smooth forehead as she noticed that he appeared to have more to occupy his thoughts than her appearance. She waited until he was standing in front of the roaring log fire before she spoke.

"What did you discover, Adam? You have bad news, haven't you?"

He shook his head, his eyes admiring her frankness. "Not bad news—disturbing, perhaps. I don't know, I need your opinion on that. But it is not as simple as I thought it might be." He sat down on an armchair in front of the fire and beckoned Sybella to do the same. When she was seated, he resumed quietly.

"I have had a complete report from headquarters, Sybella. There is not even the remotest possibility that your assailant was another French agent. Now I want you to think carefully what happened yesterday."

"If that man was not connected in some way with Julian," she spoke each word slowly and deliberately, "then he must have had some other reason for attacking me." She opened her eyes wide with horror as the possibility presented itself. "But that is impossible! What reason could there be? Adam, it cannot be as you say!''

''Sybella, couldn't it be that you were mistaken?'' His voice was warm with affection. ''It could well have happened. You had suffered a grievous shock followed by three days of anxious waiting and this murderous attack on top of it all could quite understandably have acquired a false image—''

''Just what are you trying to tell me? That I imagined it all?''

''Don't be so prickly! Dammit, I'm merely trying to point out to you that you might possibly have misinterpreted this man's motives. He may have been wanting to steal your money and nothing else!''

''No.''

''It is possible. I have been making enquiries and there has been an uncommon amount of local highway robbery these past weeks.''

''No, it is *not* possible!''

''Very well, I shall assume that you are right.'' He jerked himself to his feet irritably. ''In that case someone, for reasons completely obscure, wishes to see you . . .''

''Dead!'' she finished miserably.

He looked at her for a moment thoughtfully, his earlier annoyance short-lived. ''Or frightened,'' he murmured, half to himself. ''Sybella, the quarrel you heard between your cousin and Barbara Fallon on the night of the murder, can you recall exactly what was said?''

"Not exactly—I can recall the meaning of what was said."

"That will do. Go on, tell me."

"They were quarrelling over me, Adam. Mrs. Fallon was objecting to the marriage."

"Yes, yes, but didn't he tell her that there was no reason why their relationship could not continue on as it had always done?"

"Yes. After that he warned her to stop threatening him, and he told her that his business with me was his affair."

"That's it! His business with you! What business?" Adam's voice was bright with eagerness.

Sybella stared at him in bewilderment. "Surely he meant our marriage, didn't he?"

"Possibly." He shook his head. "No, it doesn't sound right somehow. There was something else, Sybella," he caught her hands in his. "I am going to London. I believe Barbara Fallon may possibly be able to shed a little light in our darkness."

"About what?" She looked at him blankly.

"That is what I intend to find out. Now, have you got her address in London?"

"I imagine Beatie knows it."

"Find out what it is, will you? I should like to leave at once."

"Yes. Adam." She paused, still making up her mind, and took a deep breath. "Adam, I am going with you."

"To London? No, Sybella, you are not."

"Adam, my trunk is already packed, remem-

139

ber? I can leave immediately. I shan't delay you."

"My dear girl, I have not the slightest intention of taking you with me, with or without a trunk."

"I would feel safer if I could be with you."

"You might feel safer but that would not necessarily make it safer."

"I have never heard of anyone ever being murdered at Grillons! Besides, I have a very good reason for wanting to go. Ronnie still does not know about Julian's death. It would be quite unforgivable to allow him to read about it in a newspaper first."

"I assure you Ronald will hear the news from me personally. Now, be a good girl and ask Beatie for that address."

"Adam, you might as well allow me to go with you because I have made up my mind to go anyway."

"You are a wayward, obstinate, and particularly irritating female—did you know that? I shall allow you fifteen minutes, no longer. Is that understood?"

"I shall be ready." With a vivid smile she flew to the door and almost knocked Beatie down in her haste as she sped down the narrow corridor.

"Oh, Beatie, quickly!" she gasped. "I must have the address of Mrs. Fallon in London, and—oh, you must help me change my dress! I shall explain everything to you whilst I am getting ready.'' She was already at the foot of the staircase.

"There is no need to explain anything, I heard every word.'' Disapproval vibrated from every muscle of Beatie's sparse frame.

"Beatie, you should be ashamed of yourself! Eavesdropping!''

"Don't you talk to me about shame, young lady!''

"Darling, Beatie, I have not the time to talk to you about anything at the moment. Now, please do help me get ready.''

"You are not going to London with Mr. Brady alone, Sybella. I shall go with you!''

"Beatie, I not only do not have the time to wait for you. I also do not have sufficient money to take you!''

Beatie set her thin lips in a straight line. "I have a little money of my own. I also have Barbara Fallon's address!''

Thirty minutes later a surprisingly subdued trio climbed into Adam Brady's carriage and set out on the long, tiring journey to London.

Even though the hour was late when they finally reached London, the streets beneath the haphazardly flickering oil lights were still thronged with people, the noise and clamour of traffic deafening after the many hours they had spent travelling through the quiet countryside. As their carriage slowly threaded its course through the snare of traffic, Sybella's eyes were sparkling with excitement, all former weariness forgotten, as she craned forward to catch a glimpse of a smart, bow-windowed shop or the occupants of a gilded carriage passing in the other direction. The cold, smoky night air was hideous with the discordant jangle of street organs, tambourines and fiddles, the cries of vendors extolling the rival merits of chestnuts or baked fruits from the warm glow of their charcoal braziers. Sybella drank it all in, loving every moment of it, and watching her, Adam Brady all but forgot the grim reason for their journey.

They drove directly to Grillons Hotel in Albemarle Street, Mayfair, where Adam attended to all details for their stay. Then with the understanding that he would present himself in the lounge at ten o'clock the following morning, he bade them a restful night and proceeded to his own establishment not far distant in Brook Street.

At ten o'clock precisely Sybella received word in her rooms that Mr. Brady was awaiting her pleasure in the lounge and she hurried downstairs to find him the cynosure of a score of highborn, admiring eyes. She swept up to him proudly and almost swooned with delight as she glimpsed the feline envy mirrored on every countenance.

"What sort of a hotel is this?" he whispered hoarsely. "It is like a home for old ladies."

Sybella smiled. "A woman might disagree with you."

"What does that cryptic remark signify?"

"I would not dream of telling you. You are far too overbearingly conceited as it is." She hugged his arm as he guided her towards the door. When they reached the street, she clapped her hands together with a little exclamation of delight.

"Oh, Adam, I prayed last night for a lovely day and just look at that blue, blue sky! Is it really very selfish of me?"

"Not very." Adam smiled at her little-girl pleasure. "Besides, you have the whole of London to share it with you. I think it is rather commendable of you."

"Adam, did you glimpse the ladies in that carriage? They must have been Royalty at *least*! And just look at the number of bandboxes that young girl is carrying! Do you think they are model bonnets? Bond Street is just around the corner. Oh, Adam, isn't London the most wonderful place! How can you bear to live anywhere else!" She prattled on excitedly and Adam, for whom Mayfair had long since been robbed of its magic by the fashionable boredom of its habitues, saw it all anew through her eyes.

"Adam, we shall have a delightful day even though we do have to find that Mrs. Fallon, though I am sure I cannot imagine what possible information she can give us."

"We shall see." He looked at her with a sudden grin. "Don't tell me that old dragon, Beatie, has allowed you to spend the whole day with me unattended?"

143

"Beatie had some shopping she wanted to do. Besides, I don't think she believes any harm can befall me in the daytime."

"Then we must not allow her to find out that I am at my most dangerous between two and three o'clock in the afternoon, must we?"

The address where they hoped to find Barbara Fallon was in Chiswick, a pleasantly rural locality about half an hour's journey outside London. They reached the neighbourhood shortly before midday and after making enquiries at the local public house were soon given directions which took them halfway along a winding cart track leading to the river. Here, partially hidden by a church, they discovered St. Matthew's Yard, a delightful little cul-de-sac, which in summertime would have been completely concealed behind trees. It contained three identical whitewashed cottages, deeply thatched, with tiny latticed windows. The furthest one was that which they sought.

The door was opened by a woman who, in outward appearance at least, was instantly recognizable as Barbara Fallon's sister. She was possibly ten years older and her hair was silvered but her politely formal manner and soft voice were surprisingly the same.

"We are looking for Mrs. Barbara Fallon." Adam smiled disarmingly. "Does she live here?"

"She stays here sometimes." The woman hesitated, still standing in the doorway. Behind her a log fire was burning invitingly. "I am her sister."

"Is your sister here at present?"

She hesitated further and Sybella said quickly, "I am Sybella Howard from Rivers House. We would like to see your sister if we may. We have some news for her relating to my cousin, Lord Rivers."

"News? I'll fetch her." She moved away from the door before returning with a little smile of apology. "You'd best come inside out of the cold."

The room they entered was tiny but neat and comfortably furnished. Within a few seconds of her sister's departure Barbara Fallon entered the room alone. She nodded her head politely to Sybella, rather as if she had just entered the sitting room at Rivers House, then looked directly at Adam. As soon as Sybella had made the necessary introductions, Mrs. Fallon addressed them both. "My sister told me you have a message from Lord Rivers."

"Not a message, Mrs. Fallon. Instead, unhappy news, I fear." Adam spoke.

"Has he been taken ill? I don't understand why you should come to me." Though there was some indication of agitation in her voice, her expression was completely noncommittal.

"I am afraid Lord Rivers is dead. He died from injuries sustained in a fall from a horse."

Barbara Fallon did not answer. She lowered her head slightly to one side, a mannerism Sybella had noted on many occasions and one which completely succeeded in hiding her thoughts. When she faced them again, only the flutter of nervousness in her entwined fingers betrayed any emotion whatsoever.

"It was especially kind of you to come and tell me this," she said quietly. "I do appreciate it." She studied Adam's face candidly. "Lord Rivers was such a fine horseman—I feel sure it must have been a most unlucky accident."

"Yes, indeed it was." Adam hesitated. "Now that we are here, Mrs. Fallon, it may well be that you can erase a certain perplexity from Miss Sybella's mind."

"Me?" Mrs. Fallon raised her eyebrows but made no attempt to question further, merely waited for Adam to continue.

"Perhaps. I think you may possibly have known Lord Rivers better than most people, Mrs. Fallon. For that reason you might well be in a position to tell us what his plans were concerning Miss Sybella."

"Plans?" She allowed herself to show the trace of a smile and looked directly at Sybella. "He planned to marry her, of course!"

"Of course. But why? Can you tell me that, Mrs. Fallon?"

She said nothing for a moment, then she shrugged her shoulders. "I have nothing to hide and I've no wish to cause ill-feeling. Besides, what you do not yet know, you will very soon find out for yourselves without any help from me, so I may as well tell you now. Yes, I know why Lord Rivers was marrying his cousin. He told me often enough, though perhaps not as bluntly as I am going to put it. He was marrying her for her money."

"For my *money*!" Sybella stared at her incredulously and then she started to laugh. "Oh, Mrs. Fallon, please forgive my rudeness but if you only knew how completely misinformed you have been!"

"No, Miss Howard. You are the one who has been misinformed and from the expression I see now on your face, I suspect you have been misinformed all of your life."

Sybella turned to Adam with a shrug of disbelief but he was concentrating intently upon Mrs. Fallon's next words.

"As your guardian, Lord Rivers had always had complete control of your investments, as you know. During this past year he lost the greater part of his own fortune in a bad business venture and in attempting to recoup his losses he threw away all of yours as well. He was desperate for money, I have seen proof of that, and he was prepared to go to any lengths to get it."

"But if he had already stolen my money—" Sybella looked at the woman helplessly.

"There still remained a trust of twenty thousand pounds which you would inherit upon your twenty-first birthday. I do not know whether he ever intended that you should know the extent of this fortune, but if he did, he knew that as your husband you would never question him his control of your money just as you had never

147

done while he was your guardian."

"I can't believe it! Are you sure? Why, even my aunt—even Beatie didn't know."

"It is true. You can find out for yourself this afternoon. Why should I lie?" She looked away as if she considered the visit at an end and Sybella moved slowly towards the door. She hesitated on the threshold before glancing back.

"Mrs. Fallon, is that the reason why you left Rivers House?" she asked softly.

"I loved your cousin, Miss Howard." She lifted her head defiantly. "I believe I would have had no scruples where you were concerned and he had never suggested that I should go. Yes, that is why I left. I finally found out I had been in love with a man who had never even existed except in my imagination. Julian Rivers was a selfish, contemptible man, who deserved to die."

Adam gently touched Sybella's arm, and with a quiet inclination of his head to Mrs. Fallon, he drew her out of the cottage. Neither of them spoke until Adam had closed the gate of St. Matthew's Yard behind them and had helped Sybella up into the carriage.

"What does it all mean, Adam?" she whispered. A wind had sprung up and was blowing cold across from the river and she shivered miserably.

"It means, Miss Sybella Howard, that you are probably, at this moment, the most eligible heiress in the whole of England! Had you thought of that?"

"Stop it! It's madness! I don't believe anything she said!" She paused. "But why should she lie?" she whispered.

"Why indeed!"

Adam concentrated upon the road and it wasn't until they had been travelling for about ten minutes that Sybella spoke again. "Adam, you knew that Julian had no money, don't you?" He nodded and she went on, "But you never knew anything about my inheritance, did you?" He shook his head once more, his eyes straight ahead on the road. "Did you suspect it?"

"Possibly."

"Adam, tell me honestly, do you believe this money is connected with—with that man? *Do you*?"

"Yes, Sybella."

"*But how*? How could anyone know if I myself didn't? Julian would never have told anyone, would he?"

"Barbara Fallon knew, so could others have known."

"But who?"

"That is what I have to find out."

"How? By waiting until someone puts a knife in my back?"

Adam grinned. "I'd never be so unchivalrous."

"I can't go into hiding for the remainder of my days!" she told him stonily.

"I wouldn't expect you to. But you could go into hiding for the next twenty-four hours or until I send for you, couldn't you? Come, cheer up! You are a very rich young lady and nobody has ever been murdered at Grillons, you told me that yourself!''

Beatie had not yet returned from her shopping expedition when Sybella arrived back at the hotel. She let herself into the room and threw off her cloak and bonnet, her mind awhirl with doubts and confusion. She heard movement in the passage outside and she immediately crossed and turned the key in the door. It wasn't until she had made the action and heard further movement and then the voices of a man and a woman as they passed on by that she realized how nervous she was and how easily it would be for her to be a victim of her own imagination. She walked slowly across to her bed and sat down heavily, listening to the noise of the traffic drifting up from the street below. Finally she laid her head down upon the pillow and wearily closed her eyes. She went to sleep not long afterwards, still attempting to envisage twenty thousand pounds laid out on a table in front of her.

It was quite dark in the room when she awoke to sharp knocking on the door and her own name being called. Stumbling in the unfamiliar room, she finally reached the door and fumbled with the key.

Beatie eyed her suspiciously. "You scared me out of my wits!" she exclaimed. "Why were you so long in answering? And why are you in darkness?"

"I was asleep."

"Asleep?" Beatie busied herself with the lamps. "Aren't you well?"

"Surely there isn't anything particularly sinister about being tired?" Sybella's voice was irritable.

"I never said there was!" Beatie sniffed but good humour got the better of her and she imparted the information she was so eagerly longing to share. "Who do you think I saw in Bond Street, Sybella? Cousin Ronald! My, you should have seen his face when he recognized me. I've never seen a man look so astonished."

"You told Ronnie I was here?" Sybella caught her breath sharply.

"Of course I did. He seemed most hurt you had not yet been to visit him—and I cannot say I understand that myself." She lit the last lamp. "Did you find Mrs. Fallon?"

Sybella hesitated and the answer she was about to give Beatie died in her throat. "No," she lied and she felt herself blush with shame for the impulse that had made her say it. "I believe I shall freshen myself for dinner, Beatie," she murmured abruptly and crossed to the small adjoining dressing room without another word.

She was still in the dressing room when she heard the knock on the door outside followed by Beatie's murmured conversation with someone in the other room. When she entered the bedroom, the hotel receptionist was just closing the door behind him.

"Oh, there you are." Beatie turned and saw her. "That was a message for you, Sybella.

There is a man asking for you in the lobby.''

"Who?''

"I am coming to that. He did not give a name but he said that Mr. Brady asked him to convey you to his rooms.''

Sybella hesitated, then she picked up the same cloak she had discarded that afternoon. "I will go downstairs right away.''

"I will go with you.''

"No, I shall be perfectly all right. Brook Street is only a few minutes from here.''

"It doesn't signify. It isn't proper.''

"Don't fuss. Fetch me my yellow bonnet.''

The lobby was empty except for one man, a tall, pleasantly featured man, rather swarthy of complexion, holding a tall, mohair hat loosely between his fingers, a burgundy-coloured greatcoat slung casually across his shoulders. He was standing in the centre lobby watching the staircase and he moved forward the moment Sybella appeared.

"Miss Howard?'' Sybella thought that she detected the slightest trace of an accent in his well-modulated voice.

"Yes. You are a friend of Mr. Brady's?''

"I am. My name is Lowe. Adam requested me to convey you to his address.'' He was already steering her towards the doorway.

"Has something happened?'' she asked.

The stranger smiled. "Nothing serious, I feel sure. Adam is a careful man, no? Ah, here is our carriage.'' With a slight nod of his head to the driver he opened the door and helped Sybella to enter. Before he had even settled himself beside her, the driver had already started the horses.

"Have you known Adam long?" In the darkness she could only see the silhouette of his profile as he gazed straight ahead.

"Not long." His manner seemed preoccupied and she looked at him more closely but he continued to stare straight ahead.

Her face burning a little with embarrassment at his incivility, Sybella turned to the window. For several minutes she looked through the glass blankly, oblivious of the hurrying figures and flickering oil lights they were swiftly passing. Then, with a sudden start, she realized she could see only complete darkness on either side of her. Scrutinizing it further, her eyes growing more accustomed to the light, she could see that the carriage had taken a route that was leading them to open fields.

"Where are we going?" Her voice shook apprehensively despite her efforts to control it. "Where is Adam?"

"We shall be there in a few minutes." The stranger did not even bother to turn his head.

"But where?" He did not answer again and she felt her body go suddenly cold as she realized with a sudden sickness that she had walked into a trap. But who had set the trap she dared not even guess.

Chapter Six

The horses were being driven at such a pace that the carriage jolted and swayed alarmingly, and it took all Sybella's strength to prevent herself from being flung to the floor of the cabin each time the wheels passed over a scar in the road. She had long since disposed of her bonnet and now she groped in the inhospitable darkness for something with which to steady herself. She finally discovered a loop of heavy velvet hanging beside the window which seemed intended for this purpose and she clung to it gratefully. Now that she was no longer at the mercy of every pebble on the road, she felt she might once more set her thoughts upon some coherent course of action although the possibility of doing anything at all seemed distinctly remote. She stole a sideways glance at her captor but he continued to maintain the same enigmatic silence with which he had initiated the journey and in the pitch blackness she could not determine whether he was even aware of her scrutiny. She pressed her body against the side of the carriage and strove to pierce the darkness through which they were travelling but to no avail. Unfamiliar as she was with London and its environs, she had no idea where she could be but she estimated that they had been travelling for the better part of twenty minutes.

She closed her eyes tightly to concentrate better upon her predicament but instead of achieving the clarity of thought she had hoped for, into her mind two questions that throbbed and nagged and grew louder and more urgent until finally all else was obliterated and the bitter gall of panic started once more to rise in her throat.

Where was she going? Who was waiting for her arrival? And there was no answer with which she could quell her fear.

Sybella opened her eyes as she felt the motion of the carriage gradually lessen. She turned her head swiftly to the window and, suddenly bedside her, lit by an unexpected row of lanterns, lay the flickering water of the Thames. On the other side of the carriage, set well back from the road, gleamed the lighted windows of private residences. They were passing through what was evidently a well-to-do neighbourhood and Sybella glanced at her companion hesitantly.

"Are we almost there?" she asked. Her voice trembled a little.

"A few moments more."

"*Please* tell me—am I really going to see Mr. Brady?"

"You are."

"But—I—why—" She broke off, utterly bewildered. "Who are you?" she whispered.

His face softly lit now by the passing lights, smiled fleetingly at her question.

"Nobody of consequence," he told her.

"But you *are* a Frenchman!" It was a statement, not a question and it was blurted out even before she had time to realize it herself. The effect was instantaneous. The stranger's mouth fell open in dismay and the mask of impassivity dropped instantly from his face. Then, with obvious effort, he recovered his composure. "Mademoiselle is most observant," he remarked stonily and with this final rejoinder Sybella was obliged to complete the remainder of the journey in silence.

At first the house was so hidden by trees she could see nothing. Then as the carriage drew nearer and turned the corner of the short carriageway, an austere but not unattractive two-storied building of pale grey brick sprang into view. There was no light except the lanterns burning beside the front door and no sound apart from the soft rustling of wind in the trees and the intermittent howling of a dog not far distant. With a little shiver Sybella allowed herself to be helped down from the carriage. There was no further word spoken by her companion and her entry into the house itself was conducted in the same vein for, apart from a brief nod of the

156

head between her mysterious escort and the elderly, uniformed butler who opened the door, no word was spoken or interest given to her arrival which was obviously expected.

She was ushered through a dimly lit hall and along a passageway, their footsteps echoing upon the uncarpeted boards and competing with the noisy hammering of her own heart. The walls were whitewashed and bare, the furniture, except for one Gothic-type chair in the entrance, nonexistent, and the place smelt musty as if it had not been aired for some months.

The butler finally stopped outside a door and, opening it, indicated to Sybella with a polite bow for her to enter. She forced a frosty smile of acknowledgement between her lips and stood watching the door close behind her. She waited until she had heard his footsteps echoing away down the passageway before she hurried to it and turned the handle. It had not been locked.

Her fingers nervously plucking at the ribbon of the bonnet she abstractedly held between her hands, she made a cursory examination of the room she had just entered. It was a very large room, high-ceilinged and lit by both oil and candles. At first glance it seemed not inconceivable that everything from the rest of the house had been stored in it, for the walls were overcrowded with oil paintings and water colours and, although all neatly arranged, there seemed to be an overabundance of chairs and sofas, bureaux and small tables, whilst the lower end of the room, which was in darkness, had had its contents totally obscured by holland covers. However a large log fire was burning brightly and the room was comfortably warm.

For fully ten minutes Sybella waited, staring blankly ahead of her, her mind casting about like a bird trapped in a cage. She had looked at the water colour probably a dozen times since entering the room without actually having seen it, when something about it suddenly attracted her attention and she examined it more closely. For a moment she felt she could no longer trust her eyes, for the delicate little portrait of the girl with the coal black hair and lacy white dress might easily have passed for a copy of her own likeness. With trembling fingers she removed the frame from its position on the wall and studied it carefully. In the left-hand bottom corner it bore a name and a date and with a little gasp of pleasurable amazement Sybella read the name of her father, John Howard and the year, 1780. The girl in the drawing was, of course, her mother. But what was it doing here? Who was the owner of the house?

She swung around expectantly, holding her breath, as the approaching footsteps first echoed along the passageway. As they quickly drew closer, she found herself riveting her attention upon the door of the room, her body growing tense both with fear and longing for the moment that would finally rid her of the burden of uncertainty. Then the footsteps drew level with the door and died.

With pounding heart Sybella watched the door

open. At first she was completely dumbfounded and then with a startled gasp that she tempted to stifle with the back of her hand, she found her voice. *"Uncle Philippe!"*

"My dear child, forgive my tardiness!" He strode forward, arms outstretched to greet her, his customary bluff good humour lighting his face. "Such a joy to see you again, my dear Sybella, but, oh! such a sadness we have had, eh? Poor Julian! A fine man!"

"Uncle Philippe—I—never expected—this is—"

"Of course you didn't! How could you? Such a charade! Forgive me, my child, but it was the only method I could employ to bring you here this evening." His forehead creased with genial understanding at her bewilderment as he patted her shoulder comfortingly. "It surely seems irremissible to you at this moment but I promise you there was no possible alternative." He frowned suddenly. "You were not fearful, were you, Sybella? I made it quite clear that if you suspected for one moment that you were not being conducted to Mr. Brady, you were to be told at once that it was I, your uncle, who had sent for you."

Sybella recalled her trepidation of the past hour and allowed herself a wry little smile at her uncle's solicitude. "Please do not concern yourself further, Uncle Philippe, I am here," she responded dryly.

"Of course you are—and as pretty as can be! But why do we stand when we can be seated?"

"You do not have to entertain me, Uncle Philippe." Her voice shook a trifle but she tilted her chin defiantly, her gaze never faltering. "You may treat me as you would any other prisoner."

"Prisoner?" Philippe Servais stared back at his niece in astonishment. "I am afraid I do not quite follow you."

"It is not difficult, surely. I was brought here by one of your hirelings. I have no idea where I am or how to return to London."

"My dear Sybella, that fine old imagination you have has finally played you false."

"Uncle Philippe, please don't lie to me. It isn't necessary. I admit that much is happening that I cannot understand but there is also much that I do know. For instance, I know the truth of your association with Julian and why you are so concerned about his murder."

"Do you, my dear?" He nodded his head thoughtfully. "Your Mr. Brady has been confiding in you, I see."

"Yes, but when he tried to tell me about you, I laughed at him. I wouldn't believe him!" The self-control that she had exercised so valiantly suddenly began to crumble and tears brimmed in her eyes.

Watching her face, Philippe Servais smiled sadly. "And so now you believe your old uncle is an ogre, eh?" He sighed. "Show a little mercy, my child. Do not condemn me simply because I am a Frenchman—for that is what I am!" His eyes sparkled. "And so was your

160

mother a Frenchwoman, so you see, by rights, you too owe some allegiance to France. I think you are of an age when it is not impossible for you to consider such questions."

"I do not wish to consider such questions. The war is over. Why does everyone insist upon behaving as if it isn't?"

"The war is not over, my dear. It has scarcely yet begun."

"I don't believe you! I won't believe you!" She turned from him, her shoulders trembling. "Why am I here?" she whispered at last. "What do you want from me?"

"You cannot guess?"

"No." She turned, prompted by the expression in his voice. He was smiling gently at her puzzlement.

"I wish to speak with your Mr. Brady, my child. Until now I have had the opportunities but never the bargaining power. Tonight I possess both."

"Adam is here."

"No, not just yet."

Sybella stared back at him in bewilderment and he chuckled happily. "A charming young Englishman, Mr. Brady, don't you agree? I would say his gallantry where women are concerned is almost French."

"You mean I am a decoy!"

"Yes, my dear, you are."

"You don't believe Adam Brady will follow me here!"

"I am convinced of it."

161

"But that is ridiculous! Why, at this moment he will not even be aware that I am not in my room at Grillons Hotel!"

Philippe Servais glanced at his timepiece and smiled gently. "At this moment, Sybella, I would venture to say that your Mr. Brady is within ten minutes of being in our company."

"Adam will be too clever to fall into such a trap."

"Perhaps."

"He will—just you wait!" Sybella moistened her lips. "What will you do to him?" she whispered.

"If he should not be so clever after all, you mean?" Philippe Servais smiled. "I don't believe I have planned to do anything to him, my child. I have a number of questions to ask him, a little information to elicit—nothing more." He raised one eyebrow quizzically. "Are you by any chance cherishing some affection for your charming Mr. Brady?"

"Certainly not!"

"Of course not. It was but a thought. However, if it were so, I would be perfectly willing to put your mind at rest by assuring you that Mr. Brady's early demise is of no possible use to me."

"And what about my early demise, Uncle Philippe? Or have you changed your mind about me also?"

Her uncle frowned. "What do you mean by that strange remark, child?"

Sybella struggled to keep her voice steady.

"I wonder you could have forgotten so soon, Uncle Philippe."

"Forgotten what? Out with it. What are you saying?"

"Three days ago someone attempted to murder me. I believe it was thought I was more profitable to that person dead. I think perhaps they have now changed their mind."

"Enough!" The good humour died completely in Philippe Servais' voice. "I have been patient, Sybella, for I have blamed myself for your overwrought state, but these insinuations I will not tolerate. I am your uncle. There has never been a time in your life that I have not had your welfare at heart. If this fantasy is a product of your fertile imagination, I demand your respectful apology."

"But it is true!"

"Sybella, I know nought of this. Three days ago I was still in Paris. I had not even heard about Julian's death. I reached London barely four hours ago." He paused. "Does your aunt know of this?"

"Aunt Sophie?" She stared at him in surprise. "Of course not. How could I—"

"Then do not tell her," he broke in quickly. "It will merely upset her. Allow me to look into this thing first." He glanced quickly at his timepiece. "I must leave you for the moment, my child. I will send your aunt in to you. Have no fear—all will be well."

He hurried from the room, leaving Sybella to contemplate what he had just told her. She sat

163

wearily down upon what promised to be the most comfortable of the numerous chairs available and endeavoured to think, but she discovered that her brain was more confused than ever and the only rational observation that seemed capable of issuing from it was the fact that she had not eaten since luncheon and that she was now ravenously hungry.

She had been sitting for perhaps five minutes when she heard the fast tap-tap of a woman's tread echoing upon the bare boards of the passageway and she sprang quickly to her feet, all thoughts of weariness, and even hunger, temporarily dismissed from her mind.

"Aunt Sophie!" She ran forward eagerly. "Thank goodness you are here!"

"My poor child! What you have been put through! Oh, I am positively furious with your uncle for doing this and, rest assured, I have told him so in no uncertain fashion! Men are all the same! Utterly heartless and completely selfish! I really don't know why we have to put up with them." She burst upon the room on a wave of violet perfume and, with chubby arms flaying and curls dancing, she swept her niece along with her until they were both deposited upon a sofa where she tightly grasped Sybella's hands in her own and paused to take her first deep breath. "Now, let me look at you." She paused to peer more closely. "You seem peaky, child."

"No, I am perfectly all right, thank you, Aunt Sophie."

"Well, you *look* peaky. Perhaps it is that colour green. I believe I mentioned it to you once before, my love. That shade does absolutely nothing for you. And where did you ever find that cloak? Truly, this is too much to endure! Why, it isn't even a passable match! If only we were in Paris, tomorrow I would take you around the warehouses and have you completely refitted. I should have done it when you were with us last month."

Sybella waited patiently until her aunt's familiar chatter should take its momentary rest for breath before she spoke.

"Aunt Sophie, where am I?"

"Where *are* you?" Sophie Servais regarded her niece speculatively. "You are *here*, my love, with your Aunt Sophie?"

"No, no, I mean whose house am I in?"

"Oh, I see. Why, don't you know, child? No, I can see you do not. Well, dear, it is just a house. A house that belongs to friends. Friends who reside in Paris and they were kind enough to furnish your uncle and myself with the keys." She glanced about her distastefully. "Though I must say it is in a frightful state. I swear it is infested with mice and the entire entrance carpet had to be taken up because of damp. I fear I shall go distracted if I spend much longer in it."

Sybella had risen to her feet during the course of her aunt's tirade and returned to the sofa with the framed water colour. She held it up for her aunt to see.

165

"Louise!" Under the heavy applications of Serkisrouge Sophie's cheeks paled slightly.

"Yes, my mother." Her eyes were appealing. "How would it get here, Aunt Sophie?"

Sophie tossed her curls and with a gay little laugh patted Sybella's hand affectionately.

"Why, the explanation is perfectly simple, my child. Your dear parents were friends of this household. The water-colour was surely a gift, wouldn't you say?"

"Yes—I suppose so." Sybella frowned. Now that the mystery had been solved, it appeared that no mystery had really ever existed. She knew she should have felt relief that this was so but, for some obscure reason, all she could feel was a vague disquiet. She rose to her feet and began to pace the room nervously whilst Sophie prattled on. Sybella had completely forgotten how irritating Sophie's chatter could become until this moment, but she tried hard to control her annoyance. At last she broke in impatiently.

"Aunt Sophie, where has Uncle Philippe gone?"

"I should like to think that he had gone to see about the hall carpet, my love, but I fear the chances are remote."

Sybella stamped her foot angrily. *"Stop it!"* she exclaimed. The next moment she saw the pained, startled expression mar her aunt's plump, soft prettiness and she rushed to her in abject contrition. "Oh, Aunt Sophie, please forgive me. I truly did not mean to be rude. It's just that—darling, don't you realize what is happening? Don't you know what is going on in this house—why I am here—why Julian was murdered?''

Sophie regarded her niece carefully. Then she gave a little sigh. "Julian had always led a rather untidy life, I fear, my child. His father was quite different. A perfect gentleman."

"Aunt Sophie, did you know Julian was a spy?"

"I knew he was engaged in something rather political, dear."

Sybella regarded her aunt in astonishment. "Didn't it worry you?" she exclaimed.

"No, I don't believe it did, my dear. Not at all. It doesn't even interest me particularly. I rather feel that all of this fighting and intrigue and sending of secret messages is solely a man's game—or rather a little boy's game. They adore it and it makes them feel so important."

Sybella turned away, unwilling to trust herself to reply. There was a long pause and then Sophie broke the silence.

"Are you worried about Mr. Brady, Sybella?" she asked quietly.

Sybella swung round sharply. "You know he is coming here?"

"I know he is expected," she answered mildly.

"What will happen to him?"

She shrugged her shoulders. "What do little boys generally do when they are not in accord with each other? Either one of them gives in or else they fight. You are probably a better

167

judge of Mr. Brady than I, child." She eased herself from her position on the sofa and crossed to where Sybella was standing. "You are allowing yourself to become far too upset. I have been thinking hard on this matter and I believe I have come up with a famous solution. You must return to Paris with us. Let your uncle and myself look after you. Wouldn't you like that?"

"Oh, Aunt Sophie, you are kind to me but," she shook her head, "I could not leave England."

"Don't be absurd! Anybody can leave anywhere!"

"Perhaps. Oh, please don't think me ungrateful—it's just that I wouldn't *want* to leave."

"Then of course you must make your own choice, my child." For a brief instant Sophie seemed to have difficulty in smiling and, noticing it, Sybella wished she had not been so abrupt in her refusal. But before she had the opportunity to make amends, her aunt had made her excuses and left the room.

When Sybella first heard the sound, she thought it was the wind brushing the branch of a tree against a window and she paid no further attention to it. But when it grew louder and more persistent she realized that this was not the case, and she glanced quickly behind her into the darkened portion of the room from where the noise seemed to emanate. She could see nothing but her action caused the tapping sound to grow louder and more urgent and with a little tingle of excitement running through her she groped her way awkwardly between the maze of holland-covered furniture to the right-hand corner of the room where she found a small, uncurtained casement window. It was set high in the wall, the ledge barely level with her chin, and she could see nothing, but acting now with a speed and a purpose that might have astonished her if she had been aware of it, she grabbed hold of a chair and dragging it across to the window climbed up on it and released the window catch.

"Adam!"

He cautioned her with his finger. "Are you all right?" he whispered.

She nodded her head quickly, striving to stop her heart from soaring as she felt his hand close firmly over her own, at the same time thinking guiltily that she had no right to feel such happiness when, at any moment, someone might walk into the room behind her and give the alarm. She cast a nervous glance over her shoulder.

"Adam—go away—please! You shouldn't have come here!"

"Ah, the very pineapple of politeness!" he grinned at her cheerfully.

"No, no—you don't understand!" Sybella tossed her head irritably. "My uncle is waiting for you to come here—he planned it this way. Don't you see? It is a trap. He expected you to follow me." She paused for a moment and her eyes narrowed suspiciously. "How did you know where to find me?" Her jawline began to harden ominously. "In fact," she continued more slowly, "how did you know I had even been brought here at all?"

"Er—Robert followed you."

"*Robert*! You mean Robert was a witness to everything that occurred at Grillons after which he followed me here and then reported back to you?"

"Robert has always been extremely thorough," he agreed blandly.

"Then why did he allow me to be brought here at all?"

"I suggest we do not waste further precious minutes in pointless discussion."

"And I suggest that you *wanted* to be tricked into coming here!" Her eyes widened incredulously. "Satan's oven! This passes everything! I believe you used me as a decoy as well as my uncle did!"

"What an extraordinary coincidence."

"Adam Brady, you are the most poisonous man I have ever encountered!"

"Abuse me to your heart's desire for I deserve it all—but I beg of you to reserve it until later. Now I suggest you allow me to perform the first purpose of my business here, which is to rescue you."

"I am in no need of rescue," Sybella assured him loftily. "My aunt and uncle are not likely to harm me."

"Indeed. Nevertheless we do not have to take the risk, do we?"

"You surely do not expect me to crawl through this window?"

He tightened his grip upon her hands and grinned confidently. "You may crawl through this window or you will be hauled through this window. You have the choice."

Her eyes blazed but she could do nothing and she had to content herself by staring at him in speechless dudgeon as she allowed herself to be assisted through the narrow opening. However, when he held her in his arms for a moment or two longer than was absolutely necessary before he released her, she did nothing to discourage it.

Somewhat mollified by the hard pressure of his arms as he had held her and the pitch blackness of the night that now faced her, Sybella meekly allowed him to take her hand and steer her through the thick undergrowth of the untended garden. She had gone barely three yards however when a stone turned beneath her thin slipper and she would have fallen had not Adam turned instantly to catch her. Without saying a word, he picked her up from the ground and lifted her lightly into his arms.

"Now I am certain where you are," he told her. "I should have thought of this before."

"How far do we have to go?" she whispered, seeing nothing except the outline of thrusting trees against the watery sky.

"Robert is waiting for you at the side entrance with my curricle. He will take you back to the hotel."

"But you are coming with us, aren't you?"

"No, I don't believe I shall."

"Why not?" she demanded, suddenly fearful. "What do you intend to do here?"

"Your uncle is waiting for me, remember? I'd hate to disappoint him. Ah, here we are at last!"

Sybella's dismay was halted as Robert's stocky figure appeared as if from nowhere and hastened towards them. He nodded affably to Sybella and returned his attention immediately to Adam. "There are five people in the house. The Servais couple, one agent, who brought Miss Howard here, and an elderly manservant and his wife whom Madame Servais brought with her from Paris."

"Good. Take Miss Howard back to her hotel and return immediately for me." He urged them quickly towards the curricle but Sybella turned and shook off his arm crossly.

"I will not let you stay here," she said flatly. "Mr. Harris, are you not able to make Mr. Brady accompany us?"

"No, he is not and neither are you. Now, get into this carriage."

"I will not! If you won't go, then I shan't go either!"

"Sybella Howard—I shall allow you exactly ten seconds to do as you are told. After that I shall slap you hard. Is that quite understood?"

"Tant mieux! An excellent attitude to adopt, Mr. Brady, and one with which I am in complete accord!"

"Uncle Philippe!" Sybella gave a cry of dismay as her uncle's voice barely preceded his appearance.

"My dear." He bowed to her and stood smiling amiably at each of them in turn, a heavy topcoat slung across his shoulders, by his side the Frenchman who had escorted Sybella. "Perhaps we should make haste to the house. The rain seems to be falling quite hard. Kindly show our guests the way, please, Claude." He paused. "However, you might first make certain that both gentlemen are relieved of their firearms."

They were escorted back to the house and into what was once obviously the library although the ceiling-to-floor bookcases that covered one entire wall were now empty. As the door was opened, Sophie Servais turned and smiled genially, the last of the holland covers draped across her arm.

"So we meet again, Mr. Brady," she said. "Such a pleasure. I hope you will excuse the state of the house," she dropped the cover on top of a neat little folded pile, "but I have had so little time to settle in."

"And you have had so much to keep you busy, haven't you, Madame Servais?"

Sophie shot him a sharp look and then turned directly to her husband, who had just entered the room without Claude and was closing the door behind him.

"Please sit down," he told them. "I suggest we discuss our business amiably and at once."

"Aunt Sophie—Uncle Philippe—please—"

"That will be enough, Sybella. I suggest you recall Mr. Brady's earlier warning and sit down. Now," he smiled and looked at Adam, "let me state my terms."

"If you will pardon me, Monsieur Servais, before we discuss anything at all, I would be grateful to discover exactly what you are using as bargaining power."

"I should think that would be obvious, Mr. Brady, even to an English gentleman like yourself."

"Surely you cannot mean your niece?"

"It does sound rather crude when put bluntly, doesn't it?"

"Not only crude, monsieur, but foolhardy."

"Really? I am afraid you have me at a disadvantage, Mr. Brady."

"I am afraid that is what I do have you at, monsieur."

"Please explain yourself, sir!" An edge was creeping into his voice.

"I would say it was not merely foolhardy but altogether useless to use a young lady's life as a bargaining agent when we are all quite aware that the said young lady's life span is going to be terminated at the earliest opportunity anyway."

"What is this you are saying? Are you mad?"

"No, monsieur. But as you appear to be genuinely confused, perhaps you could ask Madame Servais to enlighten you."

"My wife? What has she got to do with this?"

"Why don't you ask her?"

Obviously bewildered, Philippe Servais frowned and looked at his wife helplessly but Sophie's tinkling laugh was already breaking the strained silence.

"This must be an example of that subtle British humour we have so often heard discussed, Philippe."

"Adam." It was Sybella's turn to speak. Her face was desperately pale as she sought his attention, but he patted her hand and gently shook his head.

"Well, monsieur," he went on, "perhaps you will allow me to enlighten you. In fact, I believe that you deserve to be told the entire story. Aptly enough it begins and ends with your wife's greed."

"Do you intend to listen to this, Philippe?" Sophie asked lightly. "I believe I shan't."

"Let him talk, Sophie. We shall both listen to him."

"Thank you, monsieur. As I said—your wife's greed. After thirty years it can scarcely come as a revelation to you that Madame Servais nurses a healthy regard for money. Indeed, her love of spending it as well as acquiring it forced you into bankruptcy during the early years of your marriage, did it not? But on that one occasion your wife's share of her parents' small fortune extricated you. What you do not know, perhaps, is that for a long time now your lady has been receiving a healthy stipend from a certain Lord Julian Rivers." Adam was enjoying him-

175

self hugely. He squeezed Sybella's hand encouragingly and grinned infuriatingly at the deadly glance with which Sophie Servais favoured him. Philippe Servais continued to listen attentively.

"I am afraid Lord Julian was tarred with the very same money brush. He had very little left of his own but he had the control of the finances of his ward and that I can tell you was a very substantial amount inherited from both parents. Your wife knew this, monsieur, and she knew what Lord Rivers was doing but she was willing to forget it so long as her money arrived on time. When Julian's avarice drove him to spy against his own country, you and your wife were suddenly partners in the same game but, unbeknown to you, monsieur, you were both playing for separate stakes. For instance, you were willing to persuade your niece to marry Rivers because he asked you and by nature of his position within your organisation. You considered it a tactical move. On the other hand, your wife was more than anxious to see the marriage take place because of a substantial lump sum promised to her in payment for her help. Oh yes, Julian needed help all right. Sybella was almost twenty-one years of age. He was desperately in debt and the only possible way he could control a twenty-thousand-pound trust fund which Sybella was completely ignorant of, was marriage."

"Why, this is monstrous! The man is out of his mind! I swear I shall go distracted if I stand here and listen to this an instant longer. Where are my salts? Philippe, fetch me the hartshorn.''

''Be quiet, Sophie.'' Philippe Servais spoke very quietly and with a little sob his wife sank weakly into her chair. ''Please continue, Mr. Brady,'' he invited.

''I will not procrastinate, sir. Your wife came to London on the pretext of arranging Sybella's wedding—although you may be interested to learn that your niece never set eyes on her aunt. Whatever happened between Lord Rivers and your wife I can only surmise, but I suspect Madame Servais would not deny that the question of money was involved. Whatever it was, it was the moment when Lord Rivers was considered an unnecessary encumbrance. By this time she knew the message Sybella had carried had been tampered with and she used this knowledge as a weapon to get rid of him. She informed Julian's intermediary that Julian himself had sold the contents of the message. That is *not* guesswork. The unfortunate gentleman who stabbed Lord Rivers to death has already confessed why he did it.''

Sophie had risen to her feet but she stared at him mutely as he continued.

''The death of Rivers left your wife as Sybella's next-of-kin and she apparently believed her only hope now of acquiring anything at all was through Sybella's demise. I do not know who made the first attempt for her but, fortunately, it failed. I am quite certain she would have tried again before this had not your planned arrival postponed it when she found you intended to use Sybella as a bargaining agent to deduce what I knew about the theft of the last message and the identity of your agents here in London."

"Is this true, Sophie?" Philippe Servais asked calmly.

"Of course it isn't true! It is all a monstrous lie that does not bear consideration! I must have my salts—I do not feel at all the thing! Please, Philippe, send these people away!"

"And allow Mr. Brady to prevent us from reaching France? And allow you, Sophie, to be charged with being an accomplice in one murder and the attempt of another? Perhaps I should." A momentary smile flickered at the corners of his mouth. "But, of course, I cannot." He drew a small silver-chased pistol from the open drawer of the desk where he was sitting and rising to his feet, he pointed it directly at Sybella as he moved swiftly towards the door. He spoke a few words to Claude who entered a moment or two later with a quantity of thin cord. Then as Philippe Servais looked silently on, each of the three prisoners was bound securely, hand and foot, to the chairs on which they had been sitting.

"Thank you, Claude." Philippe Servais bowed to Adam as Sophie hurriedly left the room without a backward glance. "I apologize for my wife's conduct, sir." He looked at Sybella who turned instantly away. For a moment it seemed as if he might speak, then his face clouded and without another word he quickly left the room. Within seconds the only sounds to be heard were the creaking noises of the empty old house and the rain as it hurled itself furiously against the windows.

"Can't we do something?" Sybella cried out miserably. "Wouldn't we be heard if all three of us shouted out for help together?"

"I rather doubt that, Miss Howard." Robert shook his head dolefully. "We would have assuredly been gagged had that possibility ever existed."

"But we cannot just sit here and allow them to escape!"

"What do you suggest we do, my love?" Adam asked mildly.

"How should I know! *You* are the spy, not *me*! You should have learned what to do in these situations."

"I shall forward your complaint to the Ministry."

"Oh, Adam, I am sorry." Her eyes were filling rapidly with tears and she bit her lip in a desperate attempt not to give way completely. "It is all my fault, isn't it?"

"Of course it isn't. It has nothing to do with you."

"Yes it is. You are only being nice to make me feel better. If it had not been for my ill-humour, we should not have wasted all that precious time at the gate and we might have escaped. But I only did it because I was frightened something would happen to you if you stayed."

"Sybella, I know why you did it but do not

179

blame yourself. Robert and I should have known better. We are the ones to blame.''

Sybella swallowed hard and the minutes ticked slowly away.

"It is true, I suppose, Adam? Aunt Sophie really did those awful things?"

"I am sorry, Sybella."

"When did you find out all those things? Why couldn't you have told me?"

"I give my word that until this afternoon I was only guessing and very few of the puzzles fitted. Then I was advised that Julian's murderer had confessed the dealings he had had with your aunt. After that it was very simple to tie up the remaining threads."

"This was my parents' house, wasn't it?"

"Yes. Beatie was able to confirm that for me."

"Beatie?"

"Yes, although she thought it had been sold after their deaths."

Two of the candles illuminating the room had burnt out and a third was flickering within a quarter of an inch of its holder. Thicker shadows were already dancing silently across the room and within an hour at most it was obvious that the room would be plunged into total darkness. The fire had already burnt so low there was virtually no warmth coming from it.

Sybella began to cry softly despite Adam's attempts to calm her and she was still sniffing woefully five minutes later when the first footsteps sounded in the house and her own name and Adam's were ringing in her ears. Eyes rounding with wonder, she stared openmouthed at the door as it was flung open and she found herself face-to-face with the irresistibly lopsided grin of her cousin, Ronnie.

"Ronnie, Ronnie! How did you know? Who told you?" Laughing through her tears, she could scarcely contain her excitement as Ronnie struggled with the cords that bound each of them.

"Ronnie, were you able—?" Adam's voice was anxious but Ronnie's boyish gaiety overrode it.

"Don't worry, Adam! We caught the whole jimbang of 'em. Aunt Sophie could be heard calling for the hartshorn all over Chelsea! By Jupiter, Adam, I've never enjoyed myself so famously before in my entire life! Aren't you proud of me, Sybie? Come, don't let us waste time, we must celebrate!"

It was still raining heavily but Sybella felt it was almost enjoyable to stumble through the dripping foliage after her experiences of the past hours. All the time Ronnie kept up his excited chatter.

"You have been through so much, Sybie, I feel I have made up for it just a little by doing this tonight. Poor Julian. What a rotten end. S'funny, you know, but even with him dead, I still cannot think of him as a brother."

The motion of the carriage was almost beginning to lull Sybella into a lazy somnolence when a half-heard sentence suddenly aroused her to wakefulness.

181

"What did you say, Ronnie?" she asked sharply.

"He was merely chattering, Sybella. Go back to sleep."

"Tell me, Ronnie!"

Ronnie looked at Adam and shrugged his shoulders in puzzlement. "I was just reminding Adam, Sybie, that I had won our bet."

"What bet?"

"It wouldn't interest you, Sybella. Purely male recreation," Adam assured her.

"But it *does* interest me."

"Well if it really does, Sybie, Adam bet me that you would all have to wait at least forty minutes before I arrived at the house and I wagered that it wouldn't. And I did it in thirty!"

Sybella passed a hand over her forehead and stared billigerently at Adam through the flickering light of the carriage. "This is beyond all belief!" she gasped. "Do you mean to tell me that you knew Ronnie was on his way to rescue us all the time?"

"Of course!" Ronnie butted in cheerfully. "It was all planned. Adam is a grand fellow. He has promised to get me into the service! He is a great gun, don't you agree?"

"Oh yes!" Sybella assured him. "A great, selfish, overbearing, conceited, loutish, impolite, and excessively unfeeling *gun*! You allowed me to endure all of that horrible nightmare and all the time you knew nothing would happen to any of us! And to think I *apologized* to you!

Oh, if only I had not lost my reticule, I would hit you both on the heads with it!''

"What have we done, Adam?" Ronnie whispered anxiously.

"Your cousin is overwrought, Ronnie, that is all.''

"Overwrought, am I? You odious man, I hate you!''

"Why, Sybie, I thought you liked Adam excessively! I thought, in fact, that you were going to marry him.''

"*Marry him*!" Sybella choked.

"That is what Adam told me.''

"Er—that is sufficient, Ronnie. The first thing you learn in the service is silence. I think you'd better concentrate upon that right now.''

"I never want to speak to you again, Adam Brady,'' Sybella muttered.

"That is unfortunate, Sybella Howard, for I fully intend to make you my wife.''

"*Never! I would die first*!''

"You don't mean that.''

"I do mean that. What is more, if and when I get married, it will be to a man who *proposes* to me. Not to a man who *tells* me!''

"As soon as you turn twenty-one, you are going to have every fortune hunter in London society ringing your front doorbell. You will never get another offer like mine. It is far better you admit that you love me and choose me now.''

"Ha!''

"You said 'ha.' ''

"Indeed I did! And the carriage has stopped!"

"Yes, we are here, Sybie. At Grillons."

"I believe Robert and yourself should go on ahead and celebrate, Ronnie. Your cousin and I still have a little matter to discuss. We shall sit here awhile."

"This is absurd," Sybella snapped as the door of the carriage closed behind them. "I am getting out."

"Sit down."

"I will not."

"Do as you are told or I shall slap you hard. Now, listen to me. I love you, Sybella Howard, and I wish with all my heart that you would agree to share your life with me. Would you please do me the honour of becoming my wife? Then you can spend the remainder of your days moulding me into a sweet, gentle-minded, genial, and tender-hearted husband."

"Oh, Adam, I don't want to change you. It is just that you make me so awfully angry!"

"Then we shall have grand and high-spirited children!"

He moved closer and pulled her gently into his arms. For a moment Sybella struggled half-heartedly before finally resigning herself to the inevitable pleasure of his kisses.

"Oh, Adam," she sighed happily, "this is past everything!"